Technically right now, Pandora wasn't his assistant.

She was the woman who had ruined his wedding. She'd chosen to cease being his employee, hadn't she? Xander would be lying if he said he hadn't chosen his previous bride based on how her lofty social position would ease his way to the top of society, but that could all be pushed to the side. Right now, all he needed was a willing party. One that he could trust and tolerate for the next twelve months.

"You want to escape the consequences of your actions today? Well, your redemption comes at a price."

"You mean like a bargain for my soul or something?" she breathed, eyes narrowed with suspicion.

"I'm not the villain here. You're the one who ruined my wedding day, remember?"

Her fingers fidgeted fast by her side. "What's the favor?"

"It's not a favor. It's a new position of sorts. A twelve-month contract. One that involves occasional travel and public appearances but otherwise is essentially just keeping a low profile."

"What's the catch?"

"In order to accept this offer, you would have to marry me."

Amanda Cinelli

THE BILLIONAIRE'S LAST-MINUTE MARRIAGE

HARLEQUIN
PRESENTS

Recycling programs for this product may not exist in your area.

ISBN-13: 978-1-335-56942-4

The Billionaire's Last-Minute Marriage

Copyright © 2022 by Amanda Cinelli

This edition published by arrangement with Harlequin Books S.A.

For questions and comments about the quality of this book, please contact us at CustomerService@Harlequin.com.

Harlequin Enterprises ULC
22 Adelaide St. West, 41st Floor
Toronto, Ontario M5H 4E3, Canada
www.Harlequin.com

Printed in U.S.A.

Amanda Cinelli was born into a large Irish Italian family and raised in the leafy-green suburbs of County Dublin, Ireland. After dabbling in a few different career paths, she finally found her calling as an author upon winning an online writing competition with her first finished novel. With three small daughters at home, she usually spends her days doing school runs, changing diapers and writing romance. She still considers herself unbelievably lucky to be able to call this her day job.

Books by Amanda Cinelli

Harlequin Presents

Resisting the Sicilian Playboy

The Greeks' Race to the Altar

Stolen in Her Wedding Gown

Secret Heirs of Billionaires

The Secret to Marrying Marchesi

Monteverre Marriages

One Night with the Forbidden Princess
Claiming His Replacement Queen

The Avelar Family Scandals

The Vows He Must Keep
Returning to Claim His Heir

Visit the Author Profile page
at Harlequin.com for more titles.

To my editor, Charlotte, who listened and guided me back to the true spirit of this story when I was fully sure that I'd lost it.

And to The Wordmakers, the fabulous band of quirky creatives who welcomed me into the coven when my words had run dry.

This book was a labor of love and a collaborative effort.

CHAPTER ONE

XANDER MYTIKAS STOOD frozen on the steps of the Manhattan courthouse in his sleek black tuxedo and felt the rush of shocked anger simmer in his veins.

The crowd of distinguished guests and eager paparazzi seemed to meld into one around him, their expressions a mixture of sympathy and scandalised delight as they realised that they had just witnessed the stone-faced CEO of a global financial powerhouse get very publicly jilted by his socialite fiancée.

'I've never seen a bride run that fast.' A voice laughed, coming from somewhere in the ever-growing crowd of curious onlookers along the pavement.

'I'm sure he'll cry himself to sleep tonight in his piles of money,' another voice shouted, without an ounce of sympathy.

Considering some of the terrible accusations that had resurfaced since his tyrannical father's death two weeks previously, as the company's current acting CEO Xander had known he wasn't the most likeable face in the media right now. But this…he felt the sting of being reduced to an object of pure scorn and derision. This was simply theatre to the masses and he had given them front row seats to his own humiliation.

The previous moments seemed to replay in his mind like a bad movie, Priya Davidson-Kahn standing frozen at the bottom of the steps in her giant white gown. His own concern and fruitless attempts to reach her through the crowd of paparazzi that had suddenly appeared… Then the look of apology on her face, right before she'd sprinted down the street in the rain.

In the handful of minutes since, he'd had his security team clear the perimeter and gather their guests back inside until the situation was contained. The details of the ceremony were supposed to have been kept strictly confidential, every attendee covered with a non-disclosure agreement and yet, judging by the seething mass of photographers being herded down the street, it appeared that someone had leaked their location to the press.

Was that why she had run?

His head of security appeared at his side, a beacon of calm amid the chaos. 'I sent a team in pursuit of Miss Davidson-Khan, but it appears that she had a car waiting for her. We confiscated this from one of the members of the press.'

The man held out a phone screen showing a brief video clip of what looked like his bride being carried by a man through the rain down an alleyway… The mystery man glanced back and Xander growled as he saw his face.

Eros.

Of course, his half-brother had been involved in disrupting his wedding. Since their father's death two weeks previously and the terms of his will had been revealed, Xander had been lying in wait for either one of Zeus Mytikas's other two by-blows to resurface. The first of the three brothers to marry and stay wed for one year took control of everything.

'Christos,' he cursed, resisting the urge to smash the image of Eros's smug face to the ground. Xander's arrangement with Priya had been strictly business, but seeing such undeniable evidence of her betrayal still hurt his pride.

'We already have a car in pursuit,' the guard assured him, taking the phone slowly from his hands as though he feared retribution for being the bearer of such bad news.

'No.' Xander exhaled, pinching the bridge of his nose where a dull ache was beginning to throb. 'The last thing I want is my security team involved in a car chase through the streets of

Manhattan in broad daylight. The press are already having a field day.'

'You want us to just let her go?'

The noise around him was growing louder by the minute. The reporters down the street were hurling out their questions and the guests inside the doors of the courthouse too. Like sharks, they were all ravenous for the knowledge of what they had just witnessed. His usually unrivalled tactical mind tripped over such a senseless change to a seemingly perfect plan, fighting to make sense of it.

He had prepped his entire team to be on high alert today, to leave no stone unturned when it came to ensuring this quickie wedding remained a secret from both of his estranged half-brothers. His ruthless nature was infamous, as was his reputation for always getting what he wanted. But somehow, somewhere…he'd missed something. The scent of failure was enough to send him barrelling through the crowd, his guards rushing to clear the path through the gathering onlookers.

Xander slid into the nondescript black SUV and slammed the door, shutting out the din of their ravenous curiosity. It had been twenty years since he'd been thrust into this bloodthirsty world where pain was profitable and scandal was currency. No matter how much time his father had spent enforcing elocution lessons and private stylists, the same reporters who had hunted down his vulnerabilities as a naïve nineteen-year-old still found ways to make money from him. Such was the world.

'You lovebirds are done early.' A singsong voice sounded out in the dark interior as the privacy screen came down with a slow whir, revealing the smiling face and grey curls of his long-time driver, Mina. 'I finally get to meet your...'

Her expectant smile dropped, ebbing quickly into confusion when she saw that Xander sat alone and bride-less on the back seat. He felt his gut clench, his eyes landing on the freshly chilled bottle of champagne and two gold-tipped crystal flutes.

'Wedding's cancelled. The bride had other plans.' Xander undid his bow tie and popped the top button of his silk shirt open, fighting the urge to rip the garment off entirely. He needed a swim and a giant chocolate dessert, in that order. His muscles were wound so tight that a jolt of pain hit him in the solar plexus when a rogue reporter suddenly pressed their face up against the tinted glass of the car window, catching him completely by surprise.

Mina's familiar croaking curse was a welcome salve to his nerves as she revved the engine and honked her horn with such vehemence that the crowd fell away. As they finally pressed forward into the afternoon traffic, the privacy glass was raised back up but Xander could practically feel the pity coming off his trusted driver in waves. He didn't want her pity, or anyone else's for that matter. And yet, it was now inevitable, wasn't it? Gossip was one thing, but scandal…scandal would be the final nail in the coffin of his plans to take over Mytikas Holdings.

As the rain-soaked streets began to blur outside the tinted windows, Xander felt the throb in his brow turn into a full-blown migraine. He leaned back against the leather seats, feeling frustration and outrage battle against the soul-deep exhaustion that had plagued him for the past fortnight.

Christos…had it only been two weeks since his father's death? It seemed like a lifetime ago now, considering the gigantic organisational nightmare that had followed immediately afterwards.

After Zeus's death, it had been generally assumed that Xander would be the natural choice to succeed his father in the event of his passing. In fact, he had completed two decades of loyal service with that exact goal in mind. But apparently, the old man had had a last-minute change of heart. Somehow Xander hadn't been too surprised that Zeus had thrown a massive curveball his way as a parting gift.

He had long ago stopped trying to gain affection or approval from the man who'd ignored his existence for nineteen years. But what he hadn't expected was for Zeus to offer up the entire contents of his estate to the first of his children to marry and stay married for one year.

Xander growled under his breath, tapping the keys on his tablet to check his schedule. He would never demand his staff work on the weekend, but Sunday afternoons had become a regular occurrence in the past weeks considering their major planned expansion into Japan was imminent. The only reason he'd chosen to get married on a Sunday was because it would have the least impact on his schedule. Unlike his slovenly father, who seemed only to enjoy the status that came with his CEO title, Xander had always found solace in his work.

From a young age, he'd always noticed details that others missed and seen simple solutions for what most considered to be complex problems. As a young boy, growing up poor in Athens, he had been an enigma, a formidable opponent on both the chess team and on the football field. There was nothing he enjoyed more in life than learning how to play a game and winning.

But his talent had recently become more of a

liability than a gift. His enemies accused him of underhanded dealings, comparing his success to that of his corrupt father.

The truth was, he just always paid attention. Couple that with his nerves of steel and, thus far, his gut had never steered him wrong. So, it came as no surprise that when faced with a seemingly iron-clad obstruction on his way to claiming his late father's estate, he had found a simple and easy solution.

Priya Davidson-Khan had needed a husband to access her own inheritance, so he had met with the heiress on a few occasions and instantly admired her professional, no-nonsense approach to their sham marriage. Plus, it came with the added bonus of having a bona fide upper-class socialite on his arm to help smooth his transition into the upper echelons of society. He had been ready for one year of socially staged wedded bliss, the exact amount of time listed in his father's will and not a minute more, before they planned to divorce. Neat and tidy, unlike most relationships he had witnessed in his lifetime.

He'd been just minutes away from victory. When he planned to achieve something, usually nothing got in his way.

But this was different, this wasn't just a snag in a contract he could tease out. This was a person. Human beings had pesky things like autonomy and free will and the right to change their minds about something as important as marriage at the drop of a hat.

His mind spun with the consequences that today's disastrous failure would have on his plans. So many things were at risk, so many chances for either one of his brothers to slide in and take everything he had worked so hard for the past two decades to achieve.

He'd changed everything about himself in order to fit into the mould Zeus had demanded of him. And now, even after almost twenty years of fighting tooth and nail against his humble beginnings to prove his worth…he still wasn't getting it without a fight.

He still wasn't good enough. He never had been.

When the car arrived at the gleaming tower on Lexington Avenue that housed their company headquarters, the rain had begun to slow somewhat. He stopped in the cavernous atrium and shook the last drops from his tuxedo jacket, then looked up, finding the towering portrait of his father looking down upon him. Cold determination filled his bones despite his exhaustion. He would not give up at the first hurdle, not when so much lay in the balance. Although now, thanks to Eros's actions, the outcome was suddenly a lot less certain than he normally preferred.

He took his own private elevator up to the top-floor suite, where he had a team of executive assistants that ran his day-to-day business. As expected, there were a few people still roaming the halls in between offices. Four months ago, he'd been summoned here from the European holdings to take the reins while Zeus recovered from his sudden illness. With shareholders and board members already seething after some of Zeus's very shady deals had come to light, the timing had felt rather serendipitous.

But even from his sickbed, Zeus's influence had still been in effect. His top-floor staff were the worst kind of pedants, enforcing archaic modus operandi and resisting all the changes Xander had tried to implement on the grounds that Zeus wouldn't like it. One assistant in particular had caused him more headaches than most.

Shaking off that familiar twang of annoyance, he tapped the first button on his phone that was simply labelled 'Quinn' and waited for the inevitable Irish accent to answer.

He felt the pressure of the last two weeks circling him again, tightening its iron grip on his stomach with every shrill tone of the unanswered call. When it went to voicemail, he stared down at the screen in disbelief. Quinn never missed a call, even on the weekend.

When a second call also went unanswered,

his jaw tightened, his mind cycling through the conversations they'd had in recent weeks. She'd seemed tense and distracted since Zeus's passing. He gritted his teeth and dialled again.

Only one person had been allowed to know all his plans for the wedding since Zeus's death— not that he'd had a choice in that matter. Pandora Quinn had been his father's executive assistant for a couple of months before the old man had fallen ill and he'd insisted on passing her on to Xander.

Zeus had never returned to his seat of power. His illness had been drawn out over the course of a few months but none of them had truly imagined that a man known for his almost super-human ability to wield power in the corporate world would ever be extinguished by something so mundane as a cardiac arrest during a routine operation.

Xander had been thrust into the position of acting CEO, managing the biggest acquisition of their decades-long history, and with that power came the entire top-floor staff, including the much beloved Pandora. She was probably holding up traffic somewhere, doing something utterly ridiculous like performing mouth to mouth on an injured bird or hand-feeding a bumble bee. The image his mind created was one of pure chaos, truly no better descriptor for the woman herself. Speaking of which…

With a touch of a button, he called in the weekend receptionist, relieved when he immediately heard the sound of footsteps. At least *some* people were working today.

The woman entered slowly, with the nervousness of someone who had spent years under Zeus's tyrannical rule. Xander remained seated, his face a mask of polite serenity.

'I can't get through to Pandora Quinn. Has she been in this weekend?'

'Pandora…? She's already handed in her resignation,' the brunette answered, her voice sagging a little when Xander pinned her with a disbelieving glare. 'I… I assumed you knew.'

Years of working with Zeus had taught Xander how to conceal his own reactions. He had just been publicly humiliated by his supposed bride and he had barely even raised an eyebrow. But with this news…he felt his entire body tense, his iron grip on the edge of his desk turning his knuckles white.

'When did this happen?' Xander asked, tapping the screen of his phone to life. 'And why was I not informed?'

'Friday evening. I only found out because I was passing by the HR office on my way back to my desk,' she explained with a slight tremor

to her voice. 'I think she waited until most of
the office had left on purpose. I wouldn't expect
anything less from that girl. There was always
something a little off about her.'

'That will be all,' he snapped, pointedly cutting her off and striding past, out into the private
space that housed the CEO's personal staff.

The walls in here were the same polished marble, with two large desk areas tucked into alcoves
on either side. The desk on his right was home
to his secretary, an older woman who manned
the phones during the week with ruthless efficiency. Her desk space was tidy and nondescript.
The opposite area, usually covered with coffee
cups, written reminders and colourful knitting
projects, was now utterly barren except for one
lonely desk chair and a single red telephone. Everything that had ever suggested the nature of its
occupant was gone.

Xander frowned at the empty space and felt a
cold fury rise within him. What kind of professional executive assistant just resigned without
a word of warning?

It was sudden and out of character, especially
for a woman who had kept a schedule that ri-
valled his own in its predictability. Quinn had
been the only one in charge of the short wedding-
guest list and the non-disclosure agreements. He
needed an immediate embargo to be issued to the

press before anything damaging could be published. For that, he needed Pandora back and he was damned well going to tell her that.

He picked up the phone on his desk, dialling the direct line to his security team and filling them in on the situation with his usual efficiency.

'I need the location of Pandora Quinn. Now.'

Pandora Quinn had been in the late Zeus Mytikas's home office many times in the past six months of working at Mytikas Holdings, but not since his death. It seemed eerie now, walking along the echoing hallway of a dead man's home. But she had one last mission to complete before she could disappear. One last act of defiance.

She had never broken a law in her life, even when Zeus had forced her to act as his spy over the past four months. She had always done her best to keep her betrayal of Xander as minimal as possible, or at least so she'd reassured herself. But breaking into the Mytikas mansion…this was most certainly crossing a legal line she'd struggle to explain if she was caught.

One last thing to accomplish. Then she could finally go back home.

The polished marble stairs that led up to the private office wing of the mansion seemed to glitter ominously, like slippery ice. The walls were powder blue and ornamented with heavily accented columns that wouldn't look out of place in an ostentatious rococo palace. A vision of a similar pair of arctic-blue eyes came into her mind, tightening her stomach into a thick knot. She threw a quick glance over her shoulder to the foyer below, as though fearing she had somehow conjured Xander's magnifying presence through sheer force of thought.

She felt her balance shift on the steps, her stomach lurching painfully as she tilted a couple of centimetres backwards before finding her centre of gravity again. Her frequent trips and falls had become a bit of an in-joke around the office, along with her loud voice and quirky sense of humour. She'd laughed along with the others at first, but at a certain point it had felt a little less like harmless fun and more like…well, unkind judgement.

She probably could have explained that these traits were a permanent part of her neurology, but she just didn't fancy trying to describe the various nuances of the autism spectrum to people who barely even remembered her name most days. If they had wanted to know more about her, they would have asked.

Working for a corporation that dealt with almost every global financial market meant it wasn't unusual for her to be running errands on the weekend. But today wasn't just any normal

Sunday. Today her boss, powerful Greek financier Xander Mytikas, was marrying one of the wealthiest socialites in New York.

Her *former* boss, she reminded herself sternly and couldn't resist the urge to take another quick glance at the sleek digital watch on her wrist. It was almost four in the afternoon. The wedding was probably long over by now, the happy couple most likely already on their way to the airport for their luxurious Asian honeymoon. Her stomach tightened uncomfortably.

She hadn't meant to reveal the details of Xander's top-secret wedding plans, or the connected business dealings. Especially not to Arista Theodorou, of all people. It was common knowledge within the company that Zeus's long-time mistress and Xander had been at war from the moment Zeus had fallen ill.

Guilt aside, she knew that this last step was necessary. She had already formally communicated her resignation to the HR department. Perhaps she had waited until the very last moment when she knew Xander would not see it until after he'd returned from his honeymoon, but she had done it nevertheless.

Swallowing past the lump in her throat, Pandora exhaled the breath she'd been holding in and began looking for the large safe that Arista had mentioned was in this office. She'd been surprised to find the house was completely deserted on her way in, so she didn't try to be quiet as she tapped and banged along the wall to find any hollow spots. A small cry of victory escaped when she finally heard the echo and opened up a hidden panel in the wall to reveal a large, reinforced steel door.

Her hands shook as she turned the dial and placed her ear next to the old-fashioned mechanism. Finally, a useful situation for her super-sensitive hearing. After a few unlucky attempts, she tried the short emergency combination from the private CEO elevator in the office, which she had never actually had the chance to use. To her surprise, she heard the pins click into place within the lock mechanism. The large heavy door swung open revealing an unlit, smallish rectangular room beyond.

The old house dated back to the prohibition era and was filled with hidden tunnels and exits, just perfect for a slippery, paranoid old man like Zeus.

Her skin grew clammy and everything within her clenched against the thought of going inside the enclosed space, but still she took that first step and then another. She couldn't find a light inside, so she used the torch on her phone to perform a quick scan of the shelves. All of Zeus's old files lined the walls and within them somewhere was the damning evidence of whatever it was Zeus had on her mother that Pandora had spent the past six months trying to retrieve.

Evidence that esteemed Irish senator Rosaline Quinn still refused to reveal the exact details of to her beloved daughter, other than to allude that it had the potential to end her long-running career. Which wasn't entirely unsurprising, Pandora thought with a frown, considering dear old Zeus had been best known for his shady deals and lascivious affairs.

Six months ago, her family had received an invitation to attend a gala in New York. It had seemed like such a glamorous opportunity at the time, and she'd been confused by her mother's reluctance to attend.

At the event with her family, dressed in all their finery, Pandora had overheard what was meant to be a private conversation between the Greek tycoon and her mother. Zeus had clearly been waiting to call in a favour from Rosaline. A favour that her mother had been unable to deliver. The old man had got an evil gleam in his eye, spotting Pandora and calling her to enter the room where they'd been arguing. She'd tried to play the hero for the first time in her life…and she had ended up indebted to the devil himself.

With that thought, she scanned the room and landed on another row of cases along the very back wall. The evidence had to be here, it just had to be. Her hands seemed to fly frantically, flipping through the files within.

The sound of her mobile phone ringing was a sudden shock to her system, making her jump and drop one of the black file boxes across the floor. But the name on the screen made her pause, frowning. Arista Theodorou. What on earth could she want now?

The woman's smug tone assaulted her ear and Pandora instinctively winced. 'Just saying thank you for the information, darling, and paying you back in kind. I'd get as far away from Xander as you can, if I were you. Being jilted certainly won't improve his temper and when he finds out you were involved, it won't end well for you.'

Jilted? What on earth did Arista mean? Her mind spinning, Pandora straightened her spine and stared down at the phone. 'I have no idea what you're talking about but I wasn't *involved* in the way you're implying. You were the one who tricked me into revealing confidential information. You got what you wanted when you found out about Xander's deal with his bride.'

She ended the call with a sharp press of her thumb, turning the screen black in her hand. For a long moment she simply stared down at the rectangle of metal and plastic, Arista's cryptic messages echoing in her ears. Guilt roiled in her

stomach as she tried to ignore the word *jilted*…
surely the older woman was lying. That kind of
thing didn't happen in perfect society weddings,
did it?

She returned to the safe, hefting a particularly
large box out into the well-lit office. The lid lifted
up on a hinge to reveal many smaller boxes em-
bossed with the names of familiar luxury jewellery brands. Sure enough, one glimpse inside
revealed an astonishingly expensive-looking diamond watch. She sat back on her heels, wondering if perhaps she should just give up. If she
couldn't even find Zeus's evidence, who was to
say that Xander would either? Maybe she was
better off just cutting her losses and running back
to Ireland. But if he came after her with legal action over the NDA for talking to Arista, she could
bring further scandal to her mother's door…

She was so completely engrossed in her own
anxious ruminations that it took a moment for
her to register the faint sound of movement in the
room behind her. Almost as though some part of
her brain knew what she would find, she turned
her head centimetre by centimetre, then felt the
breath freeze in her lungs as she was pinned by
a familiar ice-blue gaze.

'Hello, Quinn.'

Xander stood in the office doorway, his wide
frame becoming very still as his eyes scanned

the room, moving over her armful of treasures, and came to a stop upon the wide-open safe door. 'Am I interrupting something?'

Pandora became aware of three things at once. One, Xander Mytikas was absolutely devastating in a tuxedo. Two, he was staring at the mess of files behind her on the floor of the safe and was probably going to have her arrested for breaking and entering. And three, he should be on his honeymoon right now but he wasn't even wearing a wedding ring.

'Is this the reason you resigned?' Xander's voice was deceptively calm as he took one slow step into the room. 'Because you planned to hit the jackpot and run?'

Pandora shook her head, her mouth suddenly unable to form words as she took one equal step backwards, her eyes darting back towards the mess in the safe again before she could stop herself. Almost in slow motion, her eyes snagged on a particular label and she felt her jaw sag. There it was: her mother's maiden name in stark black lettering amid the chaos of a pile of blank brown folders. She froze, her body tightening like a coiled spring.

Xander's eyes followed her gaze towards the safe, his mouth twisting with anger.

'Don't. Move.'

His voice was a low warning, but she couldn't

think of anything but retrieving that file. That had to be it, the evidence that Zeus had taunted her with for months. Giving her awful task after awful task to complete, forcing her to betray her own morals with lies and deceit, then still dangling it out of her reach like a carrot. She was done with being kept under someone else's control.

Six months of playing the part of the quiet, obedient executive assistant came crashing to the forefront of her limits and she knew she wouldn't obey Xander's command. She had come here to set herself and her mother free and she wasn't giving up without a fight. Before she could think about it, she bolted across the room.

Her smooth-soled shoes were slippery on the hard wood, setting her into a rather inelegant slide through the safe door, where she quickly launched herself on top of the files, grasping for the one she needed. She stood up and turned to run back out at the exact same time that two heavy hands gripped her shoulders.

Perhaps it was the darkness of the small space, or the painful adrenaline of the entire afternoon spiking her reflexes, but she felt something rise up within her, her body reacting to the uninvited touch in pure self-preservation. Time seemed to switch to slow motion as she watched her own small fist rise up in an elegant arc then fall, aiming a sucker punch directly at Xander Mytikas's handsome patrician nose.

His guttural grunt as he skilfully avoided the blow filled her ears, bringing instant shame that she'd even tried to hit him. And then they were both falling.

She heard herself squeak, sprawling backwards on the floor with the file underneath her back. She looked up and found herself pinned by that arctic-blue gaze once again. He loomed over her, his chest only inches from her own, and for a split second nothing existed but the twin sounds of their heartbeats thrumming in time. His breath fanned over her, his nostrils flared and pupils wide and dark with what had to be deep, incredulous anger.

Xander finally opened his mouth to speak, but was interrupted by the room suddenly getting darker. Pandora tensed, turning her face just as the last sliver of bright light from the office disappeared and the safe door slid shut with a bang.

CHAPTER TWO

XANDER'S BODY TENSED, pressing his weight down upon her for a split second before he was launching himself up and she could hear him rushing for the door. Her body felt a brief moment of loss at his departure before she stood up too, hands out grasping at the darkness to feel her way. She heard the harsh pounding of a fist against metal.

'Damn it,' he growled. 'Now look what you've done.'

'Me?' Pandora squeaked. 'You're the one who chased me in here.'

'Because you broke into my father's safe,' he hissed, sounding closer this time. The scraping of metal came next as he fumbled around, before he cursed softly.

'My phone is on the desk,' she said quietly. 'Have you got yours?'

'If I had my phone, do you think I would have spent the past five minutes trying to find an interior release mechanism?'

The darkness was absolute, the kind of dark that weighed in upon you, playing tricks on your senses. She sensed Xander move away from the door, his silk tuxedo trousers making a soft hissing sound as he continued to inspect the perimeter of their new prison cell. Suddenly, the small room was lit up by a dim artificial light. The one she'd failed to find earlier.

Xander stood a few steps away, his gaze one of barely restrained fury as he leaned back against the wall. 'It seems that we are stuck in here until my driver realises that I'm taking too long and calls Security. But I suppose I should be grateful for the privacy.'

Her mind tripped over his words, wondering why he'd be grateful for such a terrible accident. But then she noticed the dark intent in his gaze as he pulled out a chair from the side wall and slid it to the centre of the safe where the weak lighting was brightest.

'Take a seat, Quinn. We're not going anywhere for a while.'

She eyed the chair, but really the cold stone floor was a poor alternative, and they were going to have to have this conversation one way or another. She walked towards him, feeling his eyes inspect her in that intent way they always did. Only today, their icy blue depths were filled with mistrust and disappointment. Guilt threatened to choke her.

'I'll take this.' He gestured to the file she'd forgotten she'd tucked under one arm.

Before she had a moment to react, Xander reached out and grabbed it. She stared down in horror, trying and failing to conceal her reaction. She moved past him, her body seeming to act of its own volition and focused solely on self-preservation as she walked to the furthest end of the safe. Xander Mytikas was not a danger to her, she knew, not physically, anyway... But being under that laser focus was more dangerous than any of the other terrible things she had been forced to do over the past few months. She'd betrayed her own morality enough to last her a lifetime. And unwittingly, Xander had paid the price every time. But if he opened that file...

She couldn't lie to him, not again. But that didn't mean she was prepared to look him in the eye when he realised the truth.

Xander didn't open it, instead simply placing it on the floor between them, dark promise in his eyes. His voice came from the shadows, low enough so that only she could hear his silky tone.

'You see, Quinn...technically you are no longer my employee, so you should have relinquished your security clearance the moment you left your resignation papers with HR. This puts us at a bit of an impasse. So when my guard gets here, he can take you to the police or…you can start telling me the truth about what you're doing here. The choice is yours.'

The possibility of being hauled off in a police car was only slightly less terrifying than the idea of revealing the truth to the man in front of her.

Pandora walked towards the back of the safe, feeling around in the shadows for rows of neatly packaged priceless art. When in fact she was simply trying to buy time. That felt like a pretty accurate way to sum up her life over the past couple of years, she thought morosely. It felt as if all she did was make mistakes and try to fix them, try to buy some time to unravel the tangle of the words she'd spoken or the impulsive choices she'd made. She closed her eyes, feeling the tension between her shoulder blades tighten like a vice.

She was so tired.

The effort of playing the organised and polite assistant by day had seemed simple, but it had turned out to be a Herculean task she never could have anticipated.

She was suddenly, painfully aware that they were alone together. Something that had only ever happened once before on the first day they'd met…but she did her best not to think of that time. No, that wouldn't help with her composure at all.

'Zeus promised to give me something,' she heard herself say as though from afar. 'And Arista knew about it, although she didn't know what it was. I'd thought she was being kind in telling me about the safe a few days ago, but I can see now she was really manipulating me into revealing the information she needed about your wedding.'

Xander's steps froze, even as he continued to speak in a tone that was almost casual. It was never a good sign when he became still.

'Did Arista tell you what she planned to do with the information?'

'She didn't say much at all,' Pandora murmured, her mind whirring through the facts that she had collected since that fateful mistake. She mentally sorted through relevant and irrelevant points, finally grasping the most pertinent one. 'But she booked a flight to Athens the following afternoon.'

'So she went to visit Eros personally. Well, he is her son…' Xander mused, the harsh laugh that escaped his throat in the darkness sounding even more ominous.

'Would Arista truly go to such lengths just to ruin your wedding day?' Pandora asked, needing to break the tense silence that had engulfed the space. The small echoing chamber with its flickering lights and dusty shelving was setting her entire body on edge.

Xander's sigh was part growl. 'Sadly, I have more than enough knowledge of what Arista is capable of. Her hatred of me has always defied all bounds and she'd want Eros to profit from my loss.' He turned away and began pacing the length of the safe in a way she had come to know very well.

Xander Mytikas was not just angry…he was furious.

'It seems my father was feeling extra charitable on his deathbed. What was it that he promised you from in here? Money? Jewels? Priceless art?'

Pandora stared back at him, feeling her insides tighten with the effort not to defend herself. She had no way of knowing for sure if Xander had also known about the blackmailing of her mother. And even if he didn't, she couldn't be certain that he wouldn't use the information against Rosaline just as his father had. It was too big a risk to confide in him, and so she remained silent, shrugging one shoulder and praying her act worked.

'You have to know that anything you took from this house, whether it was promised to you or not, would be theft.'

'I am not a criminal,' she said with conviction,

feeling the force of those words burn her throat. He felt it too, judging by the widening of his eyes.

'Strong words for a woman who was just caught breaking and entering. Add that to breaking my non-disclosure agreement and helping Arista to make my bride run away, I'd say you're pretty far on the other side of the law right now.'

She closed her eyes, feeling the words catch in her throat even as she tried to find a way to explain. But there was no easy way to tell him that she had been blackmailed by Zeus for the past six months without revealing her mother's misdeeds. No way to get herself out of this mess without potentially throwing her mother's entire career into chaos.

She felt the world narrow around her, bringing the sound of her own breathing painfully into focus. Breathing that sounded far too shallow and far too rapid to be quite right. Warm palms settled upon both of her shoulders, pulling her back into the present with a jolt.

'Relax, Quinn. Breathe for me.'

Xander's face was a blur of shadows, but somehow she could sense his eyes on her. Without looking away, she obeyed. Air filled her lungs until the tight sensation in her chest fell away, leaving her shivering with reaction. It was the strangest feeling, because she'd been so sure she'd been about to lose control.

She shook off the swirling in her stomach, like swooping butterflies, and determinedly stared at a point across the dimly lit room, far away from Xander. She needed to avoid this ridiculous effect his touch seemed to have on her if she had any hope of speaking coherently and making him listen to her.

Pandora bit her lower lip, looking back into the dancing flames of his gaze. 'I swear, Xander, I had no idea that Arista planned to ruin the wedding.'

'What on earth did you think she would do with the information you gave her?'

'I don't usually know what people's intentions are until after the fact.'

To her surprise he didn't scoff at her words or disregard them, he simply stared at her in that discomfiting way of his, as though he could see right through to every thought in her head.

He folded his arms across his chest. 'The fact of the matter is, you did break a legal agreement. You betrayed my trust based on smooth lies from Arista Theodorou. And now…it seems it was all for nothing.'

The words hung in the air, laced with some tense emotion that deepened the furrow between his brows. Pandora nodded once finding her voice had failed her.

She didn't know what she had expected of this

moment, if he'd ever found out an inkling of the truth. But seeing him turn away from her, tension in every muscle in his body, made the shame burn even deeper in her gut.

She had almost told Xander about Arista on Thursday night as they'd finished up a midnight conference meeting with their team in Osaka, who were out there struggling to close a crucial deal with the Tanaka Corporation. Her fluency in both Mandarin and Japanese had been Zeus's front for hiring her to become a part of his top-floor team. She had been his gift to Xander once he'd arrived from Europe, his very own Asian market specialist, privy to every call and email since he'd taken over operations in New York. Only she knew that she had been placed in such close proximity to Xander so she could act as Zeus's own personal spy on his oldest son while the old man was forced to convalesce in his big mansion.

'I can help you find Priya. I can explain,' she offered in what she hoped was a helpful tone. 'Perhaps it was just a simple case of the bridal jitters.'

Pandora could hardly believe the unravelling figure before her was actually the same perfectly polished automaton she'd strived to impress over the past few months. His dark hair was ruffled from agitated fingers and he had evidently pulled off the black tie at some point. Now the collar of his shirt lay wide open revealing a tanned, toned triangle of skin with just a hint of curling hair.

'You have no idea what all this means, do you?' His voice was a sudden ominous growl that seemed to scrape along her skin, agitating the burning guilt. She felt her own patience snap, her teeth gritting together painfully as she spoke.

'Perhaps I would know if you would damn well tell me.'

Xander paused mid-step, his mouth opening slightly. 'Did you just…curse at me?'

'Hardly a curse.' She stood tall, tilting her chin up. 'Xander, we could track her down and explain my part in it. Let me… I can fix this.'

'The damage has already been done. The information that you leaked contained changes to the prenup that Priya had not approved. She quite literally ran away the moment my brother informed her of the deception.'

Pandora felt her stomach drop at his words. Could it be true that Xander would have intentionally tried to deceive Priya like that? The marriage had been strangely sudden and devoid of any declarations of love or romance, but she had simply put that down to Xander's nature. He was an intensely private man for someone who was constantly in the public eye. They might have spent countless hours working together but she was under no illusion that she had come anywhere close to seeing what lay beneath his glacial surface.

'Nothing to say?' Xander bit out. 'No rushing to my defence?'

She bit her lower lip, trying to ignore the sensation of the walls of the safe closing in on her. 'I don't pretend to know where your morality compass lies, Xander. But I do know that you tend to prefer a more direct approach to getting your way rather than indulging in outright deceit.'

'That's almost a compliment, Quinn.' Xander paused, gathering his thoughts once more. 'No. I did not deliberately try to deceive Priya. The final part of the deal was done entirely through her uncle and I was told that she approved of the whole thing. But she clearly doesn't know that. Not that any of that matters now, considering she was last seen running from our wedding and into the waiting arms of my brother.'

'She really just walked away and left you standing there?' Pandora frowned.

'I told you, she ran. Quite fast for a woman in heels and haute couture.'

Pandora made a distressed sound.

'I never planned to ever get married and I highly resent being manipulated into the endeavour. That was actually something my bride and I had in common. It was a business agreement between us, really. A mutually beneficial one that I believed was foolproof.'

'Surely there is another way to achieve your publicity goals here, Xander. Other than getting married to a woman you barely know.'

'You think I entered into a whirlwind marriage just to get a line in the papers?' His stunned laugh was laced with a growl. '*Christos*, I wish it were that simple.'

'Then why did you do it?'

'It's common knowledge that my mother was Zeus's secretary in the Athens headquarters. He paid her handsomely to keep my existence a secret from the world. Until he found out he had become sterile and decided he needed to hunt down his illegitimate children to carry on his precious bloodline.' He paused, wondering why he was telling her this. But the words kept coming. 'I was nineteen when he found me, and my mother had long disappeared, so when he offered me a chance to make something of myself I took it. I joined the company and worked my way up from the bottom. I jumped through every hoop he asked of me until I reached the top of the pecking order and he accepted me as his right-hand man, running the European arm of the business. And then what does that bastard do, even after I fly over here and hold everything together while he's ill? He offers up the legacy that I rightfully earned, as a prize to be won.'

'This…the wedding…it's all because of Zeus?'

'He left a will. A very detailed one, in fact. The first of his three illegitimate sons to marry and stay married for one year…takes everything.'

'And your brothers?' she asked. 'They know about this stipulation in the will?'

'Yes. Like me, Eros always vowed never to marry. He never cared about the fortune but if given the chance to exact revenge on me… Let's just say I need to find a replacement bride fast or admit defeat.'

'I'll do it,' she said quickly, then froze, her mouth sagging open for a moment before she slapped a hand across the lower half of her face. 'I meant that I can help to find your replacement, not marry you myself.'

He pushed away the ridiculous sensation in his chest that felt far too close to disappointment. Sure, having her offer to take his bride's place would have made things a lot easier, but he could never have accepted. This was Quinn he was talking to here. Apart from the fact that he had just uncovered that she was completely untrustworthy, she was his employee, and employees were strictly off limits for romantic relationships in Xander Mytikas's book. Even fake relationships.

But…a small voice within him piped up, she had resigned. Technically right now, she wasn't his assistant. She was the woman who had ruined his wedding and broken into his father's home for reasons he had yet to glean. She'd chosen to cease being his employee, hadn't she? He'd be lying if he said he hadn't chosen his previous well-connected bride because she would ease his way to the top echelons of society, but that could all be pushed to the side for the moment. Right now, all he needed was a willing party. One that he could tolerate for the next twelve months.

He paused, taking in the woman before him and feeling the first flashes of his new strategy edge to the forefront of his mind.

'You want to escape the consequences of your actions today, Quinn? Well, your redemption comes at a price, if you're willing to broker a deal with me.'

'You mean like a bargain for my soul or something?' she asked, eyes narrowed with suspicion.

'I'm not the villain here, Quinn. You're the one who ruined my wedding day, remember?'

She frowned, her fingers fidgeting fast by her side. 'What's the deal?'

'It's a new position, of sorts. A twelve-month contract. One that involves occasional travel and public appearances but, otherwise, is essentially just keeping a low profile.'

'This feels like a trick,' she mused, still looking wary. 'What's the catch?'

'In order to accept this offer, you would have to marry me.'

CHAPTER THREE

Pandora felt the sound of laughter escape her throat, coming from a place filled half with dread, half hysteria. Like the kind of feeling she got when someone made a joke and everyone else laughed but she didn't quite get it. But Xander didn't make jokes, she reminded herself. It was part of the reason she had always found conversation with him to be so effortless. He was the kind of person who only spoke words that mattered and always with frank honesty. It was ludicrous for anyone to ever think he would have deceived Priya.

He was still looking at her, awaiting an answer to his ridiculous proposal, if she could even call it that.

'Quinn,' Xander gritted, 'I just asked you to marry me. Have you no response?'

'You didn't *ask*,' she pointed out. 'You demanded. There's a difference.'

It was utterly preposterous to even consider

her as a last-minute replacement for his previous fiancée. She had only ever met Priya Davidson-Khan on one occasion, when the other woman had come to the office to sign some documents with her uncle. The entire office, including herself, had been a little transfixed at the woman's confident stride and effortless class. She wasn't just beautiful…she was the whole package. Intelligent, well bred and knowledgeable about the pitfalls of high-society circles that Xander needed to infiltrate. In short, she was the exact opposite of Pandora.

Men like Xander Mytikas did not choose the loud, quirky girls that didn't quite fit in.

She remembered one of the mornings during his first week at the office. He was impossible to miss really, him being all broad shoulders and piercing blue eyes. He'd noticed her with her earphones in chuckling to herself as she'd surveyed her latest cross-stitch project and stopped, staring down at the intricately crafted curse word decorated in pretty roses. She'd watched him for a long moment in her peripheral vision, puzzled at being the recipient of his infamous glare when she was pretty sure she'd done nothing wrong.

She'd tried to defuse the tension, asking if he needed anything. Only it had come out wrong, as happened sometimes when she was uncertain of somebody. Instead of a polite question, it had emerged as something harsh and accusatory.

There had been no mistaking the look on his face then. Irritation and impatience.

Over the next few weeks, she'd tried her best to avoid him but he'd seemed to be everywhere. In meetings where she'd acted as translator, she'd noticed he spoke in short, clipped sentences and he always said what he meant, no embellishing or pandering. In short, she was fascinated by him. Despite his clear disapproval of her, being around him seemed almost effortless. A rarity in her experience.

That was when she'd begun to feel that familiar pull, like when she'd first discovered a new language as a child and begun learning it, decoding and absorbing it into herself.

It was completely inappropriate and yet, she became hyperaware of him. Dangerously so. After the years she'd spent being told by teachers and therapists to tone down the more intense facets of her autistic traits, she now tended to be rather pointed in letting her fixations have free rein. But she'd never felt the pull towards another human being before. At least, not a nonfictional one.

If her unwanted attraction to him meant working together had been almost unbearable...anything more would likely break her spirit entirely.

'You can't ask me to do this. I will help you find a replacement, someone more appropriate. Someone...' Someone who is not me. God, anyone but me.

He leaned his tall frame against the shelving. When he finally spoke, there was a calm to his voice that hadn't been there before. A cool determination that made her stomach twist.

'I've already thought through the probabilities of every other solution to this problem. Quinn, it has to be you.'

His words hit her squarely in the chest and for a moment she was floating, watching this surreal scene from above. Situations like this belonged on a cinema screen, not in real life. *It has to be you.* That was almost a declaration from a man who barely even muttered goodbye to her at the end of the day.

She caught herself at the ridiculous thought. It wasn't as if he'd said, 'Quinn, you're my only hope,' or begun chanting that her very existence completed him. This was a very serious real-life issue, not something she could dress up as a romantic movie moment.

But then, of course, like most of the vaguely nice things that Xander said to her, he went straight ahead and ruined it.

'You've already betrayed me once so at least

I know where I stand with you. Better the devil I know, et cetera.'

'Just to be clear, I'm the devil in this situation?' she said dryly.

He folded his arms, surveying her with an air of impatient superiority that did nothing to soften the swirl of chaotic emotions inside her chest.

'I can't do this, Xander. Perhaps this is how situations are settled among high-society rich people but you're asking me to marry you as part of some kind of illicit bargain. It's highly improper. Probably illegal.'

'What was illegal was you breaking in here to steal from me. Not to mention breaking your NDA to talk to Arista.' He remained still…an ominous statue half bathed in shadows. 'This is an opportunity to redeem yourself. After the part you played in recent events, this is the only repayment I will accept.'

If his anger wasn't already evident in the taut set of his chiselled jawline, she heard it veiled under every syllable. An eye for an eye. A bride for a bride.

'You would become my wife in name only, so there would be very few demands other than signing your name beside mine on the legal documents, moving into my home and appearing in public occasionally to maintain the façade of a happy marriage.'

'Move in?' she squeaked, feeling uncomfortably hot all of a sudden. 'Xander, I can't…people would think that I was your…that we were…'

'That we were lovers?' His expression darkened suddenly. 'If this is going to be believable, that's the story we would tell. That our long nights in the office took an intimate turn and now that my business marriage to Priya is off, we're free to get married ourselves.'

Pandora felt her breathing quicken, remembering some of the more X-rated fantasies she'd entertained about her handsome boss while daydreaming at her desk. The desk, incidentally, had always played a starring role. He was watching her with cool interest, waiting for her to respond, she realised. She cleared her throat, praying he hadn't developed the ability to mind-read.

'But you're you, Xander. You're…' She gestured vaguely to his body, praying she wasn't blushing. It was much too warm in here. 'The last woman you dated was nominated for the most prestigious acting award, for goodness' sake.'

'You keep track of my dating life?'

'No,' she said quickly. 'What I mean is, you've never once dated anyone in the office. In fact, I was told when I started that you have strict rules about that sort of thing. So apart from the obvious reasons why I am entirely not your type, it's a thoroughly ridiculous plan that nobody will believe.'

'I'm thinking that perhaps all my rules were blown into the dust, with the power of our mutual attraction,' he mused, stroking a hand along his jaw. 'I only escorted that actress to one gala dinner, as a PR move. In general, I'm far too busy to date, Quinn, hence why I had to form a business plan in order to obtain a wife.'

'You're telling me that you don't realise there are a million women out there who would jump at the chance?'

'I'm a billionaire, of course there are. But an actual marriage would likely involve the kind of complex emotional entanglement that I'm not willing to give headspace to.'

'Not a romantic, then.' She fought the urge to smirk, finding this insight into her boss's cool, calculating exterior thoroughly fascinating.

He frowned at her words, running an agitated hand along his jaw. 'I need you to understand… at this very moment both of my brothers could be on their way to fulfil the terms of my father's will. Mytikas Holdings and every one of my employees could be on the verge of having their livelihoods snatched from under them. I am the only one of Zeus's heirs who cares about this company and the people who depend upon its existence.'

He looked tired, she realised. More tired than

he'd ever let her see before. Perhaps it was that first glimpse of honesty that made her pause. As if sensing the shift in her, Xander moved closer. Just a step, but enough to bring him back into her line of vision.

'This would simply be a business agreement between two consenting adults.' He sat down in the chair in the centre of the safe, a reversal of the power move she had seen him make before in difficult negotiations.

'If this was a business agreement, then surely I would have some terms of my own.'

He straightened, surprise transforming his face for a split second before he nodded and crossed his arms, the picture of the polished business-man. 'Let's negotiate.'

'I have just one.' She inhaled, the air feeling hot in her lungs as she tried to calm her erratic heartbeat. 'You give me back that file and never ask of it again.'

He contemplated the slim folder for a second, darkness clouding his features. Then, to her surprise, he slid the folder across the floor, placing it at her feet.

'Just like that?' She breathed, narrowing her gaze upon him.

'I have CCTV footage of your actions tonight, that's enough collateral to satisfy me should you choose to cross me again.' He emphasised the last word with finality, standing up to his full height. 'I'm asking you for twelve months of marriage to be followed by a discreet divorce. Aside from the odd social function, we'd most likely live entirely separate lives.'

'You've really thought all this through.' Or was this the same deal he'd had this morning, with a different bride copied and pasted in? Sure, it hadn't been a love match with Priya, but the idea of trying to step into such a pivotal role in Xander's life that another woman had been set to play only a few hours ago still seemed wrong. This was so much more than mooning after her hot boss from across the office. They would be under the same roof. This would be personal.

She reflexively wrapped her arms around herself, tight enough to feel some of the deep pressure her body craved but as usual it wasn't enough. She couldn't even believe she was having these thoughts, because that meant that some tiny part of her was actually considering agreeing to his proposal…demand…threat? And that would be utter madness. Wouldn't it?

His jaw tightened. 'I would supply you with financial reimbursement to cover any losses incurred over the next twelve months.'

'You're suggesting that you would…pay me to

quit working and marry you? That's hardly an ethical way to use your boss-employee privilege.'

She was not prepared for the sudden change that her words evoked. Xander froze, seeming to stiffen and coil up like a tiger who'd had his tail pulled. The mask of calm disappeared, leaving a harshness that made her take a half-step backwards. He took two steps towards her so that barely half a foot separated her chest from his and she could smell every individual scent in his cologne.

'I am not the kind of man to use my privilege in any manner. Unlike my father, I have very firm boundaries with my employees in that regard. You entered into a game that you had no business playing. I am offering you the opportunity to free yourself from the consequences of your own actions with the added bonus of keeping whatever is in that file.'

'I'll consider it,' she said, feeling the intensity of his gaze upon her like a flame. 'I'll think it over tonight and give you my answer in the morning.'

'And risk you disappearing without a trace?' He shook his head, stepping in her way. 'I've already had one potential bride disappear on me today.'

'Okay, then,' she said, with as much steel in her tone as she could muster.

'Okay?' he echoed, tilting his head to one side. 'Is that a yes?'

'Yes. I'll do it. I will marry you.'

Xander had expected the knot of tension in his stomach to ease once Mina had alerted his security team to come looking for him and they'd finally been let out of the safe. He'd decided to transport his assistant to his home immediately to complete the remainder of their bargain. His team of lawyers arrived swiftly, having drawn up the relevant documents with impressive speed. The three men now idled around the conference table of the penthouse apartment he kept at the top of the Mytikas building, watching the slim blonde who sat scanning over each word with quiet intensity.

Considering she regularly translated this kind of legal contract for her work, he shouldn't be surprised. But with every minute that passed with the pen untouched on the tabletop, he felt his impatience grow. When she finally declared the contracts satisfactory, he loomed over her, watching the smooth flourish of her signature with probably far more intensity than was necessary.

He insisted on escorting her home in his own car, the drive passing in the kind of peaceful silence that reminded him of evenings they had spent working together. She instructed him to pull up in front of a small nondescript brownstone with a bright purple door. She did not invite him inside, a fact that shouldn't have bothered him. And yet, the fact that he had worked alongside Quinn for months and never once had he considered where she lived bothered him, somehow.

He spent the rest of the evening arranging for the legal ceremony and necessary judge amendments to ensure their marriage was completed as soon as possible. He contemplated a phone call to deliver the news, but he knew she despised verbal communication, much preferring emails or texts. She really had been a poor fit for an executive assistant, he mused, wondering yet again why Zeus had hired her, while turning in his hands the small dark red booklet that held her travel documents.

It had been a harsh move, holding her passport as collateral, but a necessary one. He had seen the look in her eyes as she'd visibly considered her options. She had reminded him of a rabbit who had wandered too far from safety and found itself trapped in the path of a fox. He was under no illusion as to who played the part of the predator in this analogy.

But no matter how cruel she believed him to be, she had still agreed to his terms. She was prepared to sign her life over to him for the next twelve months and step into a role she had no preparation for whatsoever. Her words about societal expectations and reputation had not passed him by without impact.

Truthfully, he agreed with her. He'd never planned to marry at all because he had no desire to ever become romantically or emotionally vulnerable to anyone else by tying his life to theirs that closely. Bachelor life had suited him just fine for thirty-nine years. Using marriage as a bargaining tool to ensure he inherited the company he'd worked so hard for was Zeus's cruel way of taking Xander's beliefs and throwing them in his face.

He'd been nineteen on the day a shining black limousine had pulled up in front of his run-down Athens apartment block. For a young man, struggling financially thanks to his mother's extensive debts, the sight of Zeus in his sleek five-piece suit introducing himself as Papa had been every dream he'd ever dared to hope for. The offer of a world-class college tuition and a foothold into the world of wealthy elites had been too much to resist. He had promptly paid off his mother's debts and walked away from his past without a backward glance.

He'd learned that he had two brothers he had never met. Nysio Bacchetti was a descendant of

Italian royalty with genius-level intelligence and Eros Theodorou, Arista's son, had been raised in the elite Greek social circles that were expected of a Mytikas heir. Xander might have been the oldest of Zeus's illegitimate sons but it hadn't taken long for him to find that he had not been his father's first choice to succeed him.

Nysio's powerful family had threatened death and ruin upon anyone who dared allude to their son's link to the Mytikas name, a fact that Xander had only learned of after his youngest brother had already been sent a copy of that damned will. With a paper document clearly listing him as an heir, Xander had been awaiting an imminent retaliation from the Italian. But instead, the attack had come from Eros. The brother he had actually known. They had begun working their way up the company ladder a few years apart and even worked side by side for a short time. Until Eros had left the company in a storm of scandal. A situation that his brother blamed him for, and rightly so. Guilt assailed him, but he pushed it down. Despite what Zeus had thought of him, ultimately, Xander had been the only one to remain.

His thoughts intruded upon him even after he'd gone to bed and, as usual, sleep evaded him. His mind was far too preoccupied with the rapidly shifting pace of his plans to rest. As dawn broke over the city, he was back at his desk, looking down at the slim brown envelope that had been delivered via courier. Inside was the engagement ring he had given to Priya. Returned without any note or explanation, but, he supposed, the ring itself was explanation enough.

If that video was any indication, he already knew exactly where Priya had gone or, rather, to whom. Eros was a slippery opponent and one he knew would go to any lengths to get revenge on those who'd wronged him. Xander's actions fifteen years before had shaped their brotherhood into something cold and dangerous. But the news that Nysio Bacchetti had also been spotted in Manhattan had shocked him. Nysio had no need for Zeus's fortune; he was wealthy in his own right and had a reputation to uphold with his own family. But it wouldn't be a surprise if he'd seen the will as a broken promise, and in the circles the Italian frequented, such things were not taken lightly.

Xander sat back in his chair, pondering the fact that in Zeus's efforts to pit them against one another, he had inadvertently brought them all to the same city for possibly the first time ever. Surely that had to be an omen of sorts. He sat that way for a long time pondering what good could ever come from the meeting of three bastards born of scandal, each of them united only in their hatred for the man who'd sired them.

CHAPTER FOUR

IF SHE HADN'T known better, Pandora might have convinced herself that the previous night had been a dream. There was no outward evidence of the bargain she had made with her former boss as she strolled out of the elevator and onto the open-plan top floor of the executive offices. Xander's text for her to come into the office had been confusing seeing as she was no longer officially an employee, but the more she thought about it, the more she realised she had essentially left him in the lurch. It wasn't surprising that he wanted her to finish up with her commitments.

'Good morning,' she greeted the front desk receptionist brightly. Too brightly, judging by the way the man nodded once, then quickly scurried away.

She'd always seemed to only ever have two speeds: complete radio silence or a great impression of an overexcited chipmunk who forgot to breathe between words. She remembered the words spoken by a psychologist to her teenage self that had changed her thinking dramatically. 'You don't need to hide your differences, they're what make you who you are.'

The problem was, unless she pasted a thin veneer of false politeness over who she was, people noticed. If not immediately, they always noticed eventually. And not always in a positive way.

Everything seemed utterly normal for a Monday morning at Mytikas Holdings. She had seen no mention of their CEO's failed wedding in the papers, unsurprising considering the wealth and power of the Mytikas name meant it would be child's play for Xander to place a gag order on the media about what had occurred the day before.

Still, her heart ached just a little when she thought of him being put in the humiliating position of watching Priya fleeing from him as fast as her high heels could take her. Pandora got an odd little feeling, her fists tightening slightly, whenever she thought of Xander's beautiful first choice bride. A perfect society match, he had called her. That feeling… Knowing she herself was now essentially a consolation prize for someone who had hoped for much, much better…it was sadly not a new experience for her. Which meant she could easily switch off the uncomfortable swirl of thought and file it away with all the other pointless emotions she'd accumulated in her lifetime.

She'd made her decision, she only hoped it was the right one.

The next thing she was aware of was a shadow looming over her desk and a strange hush falling over the rest of the office.

'What are you doing?'

Pandora struggled for a moment to arrange her features into a polite mask. Her Executive Assistant face, she liked to call it. Xander stood dangerously close, his swarthy features carefully blank but his eyes blazing.

She frowned, lowering her voice to the merest murmur. 'You said to come into the office. I'm here.'

'I invited you here as my *fiancée*, Quinn, not to come to work.' He made a strange choking sound, running a hand through his hair. 'My office. Now.'

His own voice was a low whisper that made the skin on her arms tighten and prickle with awareness. She watched him walk away, as did everyone else in their vicinity before their curious eyes slowly switched back to her. Someone whistled under their breath and the girl who sat at the desk next to her let out a rush of whispered questions.

She had long ago mastered the art of the shrug.

It was one of her favourite weapons when language simply was not possible. Pursing her lips, Pandora rolled one shoulder and opened up the digital files on her tablet that she needed to get his signature on. Nerves made her extra unco-ordinated, so she paid particular attention to her footing as she followed in Xander's wake.

At the very last moment, he took hold of her hand and pulled her in the rest of the way. She heard the audible gasp of her co-workers right before the door snapped shut, shielding them from view.

'What on earth are you thinking, doing that? Everybody was watching.' She spoke on a rush of breath as she yanked back her hand.

'Them watching us was the whole point. They will just assume that I have taken my fiancée somewhere private to wish her a good morning.'

'Why on earth would they…?' Her brow furrowed as his meaning dawned. 'You've already told them?'

'Have you completely forgotten the events of last night?'

'Of course not.'

'We've already signed a prenup, so it's best you haven't. I've just announced our engagement to the entire upper floor. Word had already got out about the whole runaway bride situation. They all think that now my convenient bride jilted me,

I'm finally free to marry the woman I really love. Between you and me, the board are also happy that the scandal can be spun to our advantage.'

'I had a lot of things on my schedule for this week.' She heard the words leave her mouth almost as though she weren't speaking them.

'I have already arranged for your workload to be redistributed to a replacement temp.'

Her replacement. The word felt like a whip against her already flayed pride and she had to turn away. She had never set out to work behind a desk, but since she'd arrived in Manhattan, she'd fallen into an easy rhythm in the quiet top-floor office. The thought that she could be so easily replaced made her feel strange. As if perhaps she had inflated her own sense of importance.

She wondered if this was how Priya would feel upon finding out about Xander's lightning-fast acquisition of a new fiancée. She tried to push away the rapid-fire assault of her own thoughts, inhaling a deep calming breath before turning back to face him.

'This is all becoming very real.'

'I thought that I made it extremely clear to you; I need a marriage on paper. The moment you accepted my proposal, you became my fiancée, Pandora. Tonight, you will become my wife.'

'Tonight?' She felt her breathing falter slightly, her heart giving an odd little thump in her chest at the fact he'd just used her first name. She fought the urge to demand he take it back. That he call her Quinn as he always did, and she be allowed to continue to translate his meetings and sort his calendar and hide the fact that she'd agreed to act as his wife for the next year… But of course that was impossible. She felt the blood drain from her face as a tiny sound escaped her lips that was equal parts panic and disbelief. 'We're getting married tonight?'

'I believe I explained that this was a time-sensitive arrangement.'

She felt her stomach flip, knowing she had been on the verge of complete mental exhaustion as they'd finalised their agreement. He could have suggested they get married on the moon and she would have nodded along.

'This all seems very fast…' She turned away from him, frantically trying to gather her bearings in the small space, but of course Xander was everywhere. He was all broad shoulders and perfectly styled hair in his perfectly fitting suit and delicious cologne. This entire situation was utterly impossible.

New York law only needed twenty-four hours' notice for marriages, but she'd hardly thought he would try to pull together something so soon. It couldn't be that easy for him, could it?

Of course it was that easy. He was a Mytikas.

He was the reigning monarch of an empire—if he wanted something done it would be done. She had known him long enough, for heaven's sake. Why had she thought that this would be any different?

She allowed herself to look at him then, to meet his eyes and stare. He stared right back. The sensation of being pinned by his gaze reminded her of the time she had spent locked in the safe with him the afternoon before. The time spent in the darkness trying to escape a situation she knew she had absolutely no way of avoiding.

She was going to become his wife.

'You're trembling,' he said, slowly reaching out for her left hand and holding it between his own. 'Already regretting your decision?'

There was a darkness in his tone, but what she saw on his face wasn't anger. He looked... vulnerable.

'I'm not going to jilt you like Priya did... If that's what you're asking.'

'Good, because my terms still stand,' he said silkily, letting her hand go, having clearly taken a moment to compose himself. Whatever that flash of emotion had been, he had easily brushed past it and was dusting off the sleeves of his jacket with that arrogant air she was much more comfortable seeing.

This was the Xander she knew how to deal

with. This was the Xander that she had spent the last four months infuriated by. She was already painfully attracted to that cold and ruthless version of him; if he were to start actually showing his humanity she would be a lost cause completely.

'What do you need me to do?' she asked, feeling too overwhelmed and too poorly dressed to be standing in Xander's office as his fiancée. Her plain black skirt and loose white blouse had been just fine when she'd simply been his executive assistant, but now her outfit felt like rags next to his perfectly tailored three-piece suit.

'You could start by looking a little less terrified of me,' he said dryly. 'I want people to believe that we're madly in love, not worry that I'm holding you hostage.'

'I'm not good with…intimacy.' Pandora forced the words from her lips, needing him to know the extent of her difficulties. 'I've only ever been in one adult relationship and let's just say…he had some criticisms.'

A dark look crossed Xander's features and for a moment she worried what he might say next, but he schooled the strange reaction quickly. 'I don't exactly have experience with fake relationships either, but I'm sure we can both figure out the basics.'

'Can you be more specific? Do you mean like

giving each other compliments, holding hands, that kind of *lovey-dovey* stuff? Or do you mean… more than that?'

'I don't think *lovey-dovey* is quite my style.' He raised one brow, his Greek accent making the silly phrase sound needlessly erotic. 'I'm not planning to debauch you in public, Pandora, but it would be expected for us to at least touch one another on occasion.'

She glanced up to find herself pinned by eyes that seemed darker that their usual cerulean. As her pulse sped up, she swore she could feel his gaze travelling down below her chin in one long, slow sweep. Self-consciously, she raised a hand to her chest, feeling her skin heat from her toes right up to her cheeks.

'Okay.' She nodded, tapping her fingers on the door behind her in a sharp rhythm. 'I'll do my best to make it believable.'

'I think,' he said quietly, the deep baritone of his voice a low rumble, 'that the public will believe whatever we want them to…so long as we keep to the facts.'

'The facts?' She struggled to process his words, still slightly reeling at the effect the simple idea of his touch was having on her.

'We have worked in very close proximity together for months. Long days lead to long nights. We'll just let them put together the rest for themselves. I have always valued my privacy, and that won't change.'

'Privacy sounds good,' she breathed, hardly believing the rasp of her own voice.

'Once we are married and the inheritance matter is settled, everything will become much simpler. But right now I cannot give the board any more ammunition to use against me in this war. They already want to get rid of me. I need to take control of the narrative surrounding yesterday's disaster and this whirlwind romance is the best thing I can think of in so little time. We can't leave this room and have a single person question this union. The future of the entire company rests on it. Do you understand?'

He stepped closer, reaching down to take one of her hands in his. He pulled a small black box from his coat pocket, opening it up to show a simple platinum-and-diamond solitaire ring.

Pandora froze, remembering another small box she had organised to be delivered to Priya only the week before. Dread churned in her stomach as she looked once then twice at the small silk interior of the box, assessing the contents.

She sighed in relief. It was a different ring. She wasn't sure why, but that small detail…mattered to her somehow.

'May I?' The request was surprisingly gentle, coming from a man from whom she had witnessed nothing but ruthless demands in the boardroom.

She nodded once but tensed as he went to slide the band slowly onto her finger.

Unable to tolerate the sensation his light touch provoked, she pulled her hand away quickly, then cursed herself as she saw his expression harden, his eyes narrowing on her briefly before he held out the ring for her to take and slide on herself.

The silence that followed was harsh and uncomfortable, tightening her already fraught nerves to what felt like snapping point. Unable to think of anything else to say, she simply stared at the beautiful glittering diamond and pondered the monumental shift in her reality that it represented. No more quiet evenings in her tiny apartment. No more morning coffee runs. No more predictable routine. Well, not for a year, anyway.

'Quinn, could you manage to look slightly less miserable?'

She snapped back to attention. 'Sorry.'

'I need you to act like you can't get enough of me. I'm going to have to touch you, maybe even kiss you on occasion. Can you handle that?'

Pandora inhaled, attractively choking on her own saliva for a split second before she recovered. God, if only he knew the terrible truth in his words. She had been entranced by Xander Mytikas before he had even spoken to her. It was just a surface attraction, of course; once she had realised how demanding he was to work for it had been a little easier to tone down her crush.

But kissing him… That was another matter entirely. Had she imagined kissing him? Sure, countless times. Had she ever intended to make that fantasy a reality? Goodness, no. She had barely survived her first attempts at kissing back in school, which had always been an utter disaster. She'd forced herself to kiss her ex-boyfriend because it was what was expected. But even Cormac had eventually agreed that she just wasn't very good at it.

She had grown comfortable in the quiet monotony of single life and now a Greek billionaire with luminous skin and perfect hair was calmly asking if he could touch her for the foreseeable future. They would play the part of man and wife and be forced to act as blissful newly-weds with all the physical displays of affection that entailed.

It was a recipe for disaster.

She was so used to living in this new life where no one knew who she was or what her life had once looked like back home in Ireland. Of the difficulties she'd grown up with, the difficulties she still managed now as an adult.

Here, she was just Pandora. But it was unfair to keep Xander in the dark, and there was no way she could keep that side of herself hidden away without sending herself into a spiral of exhaustion. It would be unfair to Xander but, mostly, it would be both unfair and self-destructive for her.

Biting her lower lip, she closed her eyes and took a deep fortifying breath.

'Xander, wait.' She waited a beat, until he was facing her, his deep blue eyes sincere and rapt with attention. He would hopefully be understanding, although not all people were, of course. But still, a little part of her shrank back and braced for impact.

'If we are going to do this, there are some things you should know. Things about me.'

'I don't mean to flinch at your touch… I'm just not used to interacting with you this way.' She spoke the words on a rush, her cheeks flushed and pink. She was…embarrassed, Xander realised. She was apologising. And of course, he was acting like a prize bastard.

'This is all just happening very fast,' she added, awkwardly studying the buttons at the top of his shirt rather than meeting his eyes.

'Neither of us were ready for this, Pandora. But we will have to be seen together eventually. We need to get a handle on this.'

She looked up quickly, surprise transforming her grey eyes to luminous silver.

'You used my first name again.' She grimaced. 'That just feels…weird coming from you.'

Had he been using her first name? He supposed he had. It wasn't something he'd begun doing intentionally, it had just kind of happened.

'*Quinn*.' He emphasised her surname purposefully. 'If this dislike of physical intimacy is going to continue, we're going to have a big problem on our hands.'

'I don't dislike it exactly. I just have some sensitivities. And I don't particularly enjoy kissing, but I could improve it with time and practice.'

Time being the one thing they didn't have much of, he thought with a slight frown. Practice, however… He cleared his throat, self-consciously readjusting his suit jacket. 'Would that make things easier for you? Practising?'

She thought for a moment, her lips pursing into a delicate bow shape. 'I suppose we could try it. Do you mean like, holding hands and posing for photographs? Or kissing…?' she added tentatively.

'Maybe just touching one another, for a start,' he suggested gruffly, feeling an unfamiliar tension tighten his abdomen. Call him egotistical but he'd never had to entice a woman to touch him before and yet this one seemed ready to run away screaming.

She frowned, running her tongue along her

bottom lip. Her usually fair complexion had been graced with a rosy-pink blush high on her cheekbones and her lips taunted him with their fullness, slick and inviting. A scant few inches were all that separated him from claiming that perfect mouth, a gesture that would be solely for performance's sake, of course.

Still, he was reluctant to look away, as though they both stood frozen in time.

He lifted a hand and cupped her cheek and her eyelids with their ridiculously long lashes fluttered shut. Her perfect, usually creamy skin was hot and flushed under his hand and before he knew what he was doing, he touched his thumb against the sensitive flesh and she seemed to vibrate at the touch. He'd bet good money that underneath her eyelids, her pupils would be dilated with desire.

He hoped so. He wanted her to feel this too, even if they both knew nothing could come of it. He wanted to know that he wasn't alone in it. It was simply the veil of her control that had such a hold on him, the façade she portrayed. He wanted to know if it was real, or if deep down she was made of flesh and blood and lust just like him.

That would be enough, he told himself. It had to be.

But then, his shy little fiancée opened her eyes and what he saw there rocked him to his very core. Raw desire, pure and unbidden, burned in her gaze like molten silver. Xander felt his throat run dry, his palms flexing and tightening against her skin with the sheer effort of not pulling her closer to claim that fire for his own.

This wasn't real, he reminded himself. They had an audience to prepare for and an act to maintain but if this was all acting, then, good God, she was doing an award-worthy job.

'You're so good at this,' she whispered. 'Touching me.'

Xander fought against the roar of primitive desire that surged within him like a tidal wave. He had always been painfully selective in his dating life, preferring to wait for true attractions to take hold, which sadly for him were few and far between. He needed mental stimulation, not just physical, in order to feel drawn to a woman.

Four months of ignoring the pull towards this particular forbidden fruit weighed heavy upon him and he railed against the unfairness of chemistry. Why now, why this woman?

But as his mind fought against his own rapidly shredding control, he had missed the gradual softening of the woman in his arms. Without warning, Pandora made the choice for both of them, closing the remaining distance and pressing the sweet softness of her lips against his.

CHAPTER FIVE

OF ALL THE times that Pandora had wondered what kissing her boss would be like, she had never imagined herself being the one who initiated it. She had also not imagined it being so…right.

Because that was the only way that she could describe the feeling that came over her the moment their mouths connected. As though she had always kissed him. And that was just ridiculous, right? How on earth could she feel as if she had kissed someone before?

But even before her mind could continue to worry and overthink, in true Xander fashion he took control. His hands moved to her waist and tightened their hold, pulling her closer so that their chests didn't have an inch of space between them.

He angled his mouth against hers, deepening the intimate touch and sliding his tongue against the seam of her lips in a firm but gentle request for entrance.

She felt her body begin to tense, suddenly overwhelmed in the face of the complex sensory onslaught. As though he knew exactly what she needed, one of his hands moved to cup her jaw. The firm touch served as an anchor, holding her steady. The press of his skin against the sensitive area behind her ear was like being touched by a live wire, filling her with electric heat and urging her to take everything he offered.

The moment she opened her lips, Xander growled, a deep primal sound low enough that only she could hear. His fingertips pressed ever so slightly against her pulse point, and the action felt so possessive and raw that her entire body shivered in response.

The rhythm of his tongue was a smooth invasion, deepening and demanding more with each slow thrust. Heat pooled low in her abdomen and yet she didn't pull away. She didn't feel threatened or overwhelmed, in fact she gave as good as she got, reaching up to lace her hands around his neck. The impulse to run her fingers through the crop of salt-and-pepper hair at the base of his neck was strong but she hesitated, wondering if it might be too much.

She couldn't resist. She had always wondered how it would feel under her fingertips, if it would be hard and spiky, or bristly and rough, but no, it was silky soft like down. A shiver ran through her body again and she heard herself hum low in the back of her throat with approval, delighting in the various onslaught of sensory wonderment taking over her entire body.

He seemed to like that sound, his body moving against hers. Hardness against soft.

And he most certainly was hard, going by the taut ridge that she could feel against her thigh. Just as she began to wonder what it might be like to press against him, right there, he pulled back, and she almost growled herself.

Their eyes met for a split second, as they both simply stared at one another like opponents on a battlefield, breathing heavily. It dawned on her that it had always felt as if they had been in a battle of some sort, but perhaps she had misunderstood exactly what the context was.

She had always assumed he hated her. But could hatred produce this kind of heat?

He opened his mouth as though he planned to speak, then closed it just as quickly, his nostrils flaring and his breath still coming in hard gusts. Was it her imagination or were the tops of his cheeks slightly flushed? The idea that she could make the unflappable boardroom titan Xander Mytikas blush was a ridiculous one, and yet the evidence was rather shockingly stacked against him.

Who on earth was she? She had always detested kissing every time she had tried it as a teenager in her vain attempts to appear young and popular. Before she had given up on trying to fit in. It wasn't that she never felt romantic feelings or sexual desire, it was simply that every time she had tried to act on it, it had felt like struggling to understand an impossibly difficult language. She'd been called too intense or too cold. Never just right.

Never like this.

'That was better.' His voice was a rasp as he turned away from her, taking his phone out of his pocket and tapping a few keys as his chest continued to rise and fall swiftly. 'Of course, we will need to minimise that kind of…contact.'

'Why?' she asked impulsively, then cursed her fast mouth.

One dark brow rose, cutting her down further from the high of that kiss. 'Because this is purely a business arrangement, Quinn. It's not necessary or appropriate. Practice time is over.'

She felt herself deflate instantly. That kiss had been a revelation for her, it had been earth-shattering and made her rethink everything she'd always believed about herself. But the shift of tension in the room filled her with doubt. Had she done something wrong? Had she committed some sort of kissing faux pas?

And as Xander quickly launched into his plans for their quick legal ceremony later that evening, she quickly wondered if she had been mistaken in his blush, his heavy breathing. If he had even been affected by their kiss at all.

Xander resisted the urge to check his watch and tried to keep his gaze focused on the skyline of glittering buildings surrounding him. The rooftop terrace of Mytikas Holdings was hardly the most elite wedding destination, but when one was in a race against time to fulfil the terms of a will, needs must.

He had changed into a fresh suit at least, he thought with agitation.

What was she doing?

Quinn had outright refused his offer to have garments brought in from his Fifth Avenue stylist, insisting that she could dress herself just fine. He had felt the beginning of an argument rumbling within him but decided that he would choose his battles. Tonight's brief ceremony was essentially just signing their names on paper, a means to quickly ensure the legalities of their nuptials were taken care of. When it came to their actual society wedding, she would find that he could not be quite so lenient. He had an image to uphold and the kind of circles he moved in cared very much about the details, which he had found out very quickly upon entering the world of the wealthy as a poor teenager.

He would earn back their favour now after his failed first wedding, just as he had done then, with hard work and ruthless strategy. Mytikas Holdings belonged to him already, whether his brothers were prepared to accept it or not. He already owned forty per cent of the shares through his own tireless determination. The shadow corporation he had started up five years previously in Europe had originally been intended as an exit strategy if required. But then the opportunity had arisen for him to begin purchasing Mytikas shares legally and the plan had appeared in his mind fully formed. Titan Corp was on its way to becoming his own legacy, one that he would not allow to be taken from him.

Grinding his teeth at the thought, he wrenched his mind back to his upcoming wedding. Going to the jeweller's personally had not been a part of the plan, but sending his new fiancée to select her own wedding ring had seemed a step too far, even if this marriage wasn't real. He pulled the box out from his pocket, once more opening it to ensure the matching rings were still inside. Then he adjusted his collar for the fifth time.

It was just one year, he reminded himself. And

it was likely to be the hardest year of his career, going by the malicious remarks made in this morning's board meeting.

The other shareholders had clearly been excited at the prospect of using the opportunity of his runaway bride creating an almighty scandal to push Xander out, and the only reason they were happy that he was marrying Pandora in such an apparently romantic, whirlwind fashion was that they thought the company would get a huge surge of public interest in the story. They hated and resented him for the progressive ideas that he had for the company's future because they were happy doing things the old way. The Zeus way. But that was just their tough luck, because Xander wasn't going anywhere.

The sound of the double glass doors of the atrium opening slowly caught his attention, he raised his gaze and found himself completely frozen on the spot.

His bride was wearing blue, a colour he didn't think he'd ever seen her wear before. In the office, aside from bright lipsticks and jewellery she usually stuck to her black skirt and white blouse combo. The dress she was wearing was feminine and floaty and flared out from her slim waist in a way that reminded him of an old Audrey Hepburn movie he had watched many times with his grandmother. He half expected her to burst into song or twirl.

She was breathtakingly beautiful.

He didn't know if it was the moonlight that bathed the rooftop terrace or if her hair was simply glowing. He had never seen it unbound from its prisonlike bun. *Christos*, it was so long, like shining silk that tucked behind her ears and flowed down her back like molten silver. It was a crime to keep hair like that hidden away.

Just as much as it would be wrong for him to wonder what it would have been like to unravel it fist by fist over his hands.

He paused, shocked at the image in his mind's eye, inhaling sharply and feeling a shiver run through him as he exhaled a slow and steady gust of breath.

By the time she had crossed the few feet towards where he and the officiant stood, he had recovered from his momentary lapse and calmly extended his hand to her.

She smiled at him, a shy smile that didn't quite meet her eyes, and he resisted the urge to question her again, to make sure she truly wanted to go ahead with their bargain.

But then he thought of the possibility she might leave and he tightened his grip on her hand.

'I'm sorry I'm late.' Silver eyes flickered up to his, then slid away. 'I thought I had enough clothes to choose from…but it turns out there isn't exactly a dress code for a last-minute wedding ceremony.'

'Is the prospect of marriage to me so daunting?'

'Oh, no, of course not.' She paused. 'Oh, you're joking. Well, now, there's a first.'

Then she laughed, a deep belly laugh that was likely just nerves but still it did something strange to his insides. He felt his lips quirk, then quickly cleared his throat and introduced his driver, Mina, who would also be acting as their witness.

The officiant began to talk, laying out the rules of their arrangement and all the various legal jargon. As far as romantic elopements went, he realised that this was probably not every woman's dream. When he looked down, Pandora seemed tense but focused.

When they were told to join hands, he felt the weight of her palms warm and soft in his own and he found himself fighting the urge to demand that she look up, that she acknowledge him in this moment.

He wasn't quite sure what to make of that.

The rest of their vows were exchanged without a hitch. Not once in the entire ceremony did she speak other than to repeat her vows or nod her head in agreement. The entire thing had been a staid, solemn affair. Not unlike the eulogy that had been given at his father's funeral.

Before he knew it he had slid the small platinum band onto her finger and she had repeated the action with the second, larger ring in the box. He had already been sure to instruct the celebrant not to announce their union in the typical fashion of a kiss. The idea of claiming his bride in such a primal fashion had seemed unbearably wrong considering the nature of their agreement. He'd told himself that it had absolutely nothing to do with his own surprising reaction to her eager, unpractised kisses in his office earlier. He was not about to be undone by a woman fourteen years his junior with what he'd bet was infinitely less experience than he had.

But now, looking down at the matching bands on their fingers, he felt perhaps he had been hasty in removing the tradition. For the sake of appearances, perhaps he should have put more thought into this small formal affair, despite it being solely for legal purposes. Their much larger official wedding was already being planned for next month by his events team, as was expected for a man of his status.

They both knew that this marriage was a simple arrangement of convenience, but the urge was there for him to prove the validity of their union, wasn't it? Behind them, Mina stood, offering a rather staid applause.

He felt keenly aware of the curious eyes upon them, and perhaps that was why he stepped a little closer and encircled Pandora's wrists with his palms. Her breath hitched, and he felt the tremor of her response like a roaring victory within him. Her eyes flickered upwards for a split second, but that was all the time he needed to prove to himself that he was not alone in feeling this attraction.

He wasn't sure why that was so important to him in that moment, but it was. Good God it was.

He smiled with ease, leaning closer and feeling her stiffen when he pressed a single, chaste kiss against her cheek as he whispered softly into her ear. 'A little more enthusiasm would be great, *agape mou*.'

CHAPTER SIX

LATER THAT EVENING, Pandora was trying to concentrate on the words that Xander was speaking to the pilot and air hostess of his private jet, but she was far too focused on the weight of the smooth cold metal that now encircled her third finger.

Glasses of champagne had already been presented to them both, along with words of congratulation before they were seated for take-off. Once the jet was airborne on its way to Osaka for their supposed honeymoon, a lavish gourmet meal was served. But Pandora was too wound up, too tense to truly enjoy any of the delicious food spread out before them. Her flute of champagne was also still mostly full, Pandora having only been able to tolerate a small sip. She strongly suspected their 'honeymoon' would involve meeting delegates from the Tanaka Corporation, knowing how frustrated Xander was with the team who'd supposedly been near to closing the deal but who'd failed to persuade the Tanaka family to sign on the dotted line.

'This will all be over soon,' Xander said, interrupting her silent brooding. She froze, not entirely sure if he was referring to their meal or their marriage. The thought almost made her laugh aloud, inappropriate as it was. But upon seeing the small furrow between his brows, she had an inkling that he wouldn't find it quite so funny.

She remembered the darkness in his eyes as they'd stood in his office, when she'd casually promised not to jilt him as Priya had. And as she had walked down the makeshift aisle towards him earlier this evening, running slightly late, she had seen the tension in his jaw and the tightness around his eyes. She had noticed the small hiss of breath leave his lungs and his shoulders finally relax when the officiant had finally pronounced them man and wife. And when the woman had completely avoided any mention of kissing the bride…she had been disappointed. She had built herself up for that moment, for that repeat of their intimate contact. It wouldn't surprise her if he had specifically ordered the officiant to amend the usual ceremony.

Which was madness, because she absolutely hated kissing usually. Something about the sensation of having someone's face so close to her own, having their lips pressed against hers…it was always too much. It had only ever made her feel slightly nauseous.

But the way Xander had looked at her once they were man and wife… She had felt the strangest sensation tightening in her lower abdomen and flowing upwards throughout her body.

How he hadn't noticed when she was sure her pupils must have dilated to the size of saucers, and her breathing had sped up… She had been so sure everyone would have heard her erratic heartbeat, almost as if something inside her were throbbing along to its own frantic rhythm, each beat shouting, *Kiss me! Kiss me! Kiss me!*

Of course, she wasn't so foolish as to think he had been that eager to marry her, specifically. He had simply been eager to get married and fulfil the terms of the will before either of his brothers beat him to the punch. Any single woman would have done just as well.

She needed to remind herself that she was only a hasty replacement in his world. She had simply been the most convenient woman in his life at the time. The feeling of being tolerated by others was not unfamiliar, but it was one she had promised herself that she would never settle for in the relationships she chose for herself. But then again, she hadn't exactly chosen Xander either. She had been attracted to him from the moment they met, yes, but she had always disliked his ruthless, driven nature. He was a workaholic, that much was for sure. He never smiled, never engaged others unless it was about work.

This wasn't the same, she reminded herself, quickly straightening in her seat and turning her face towards her husband. 'I'm not quite sure how to behave now,' she said honestly. 'I've only ever been around people as a member of your team, and being congratulated by them now as though I'm…important is unsettling.'

He frowned, a strange darkness entering his eyes.

'When I first started working for my father,' he said quietly, his voice an intimate murmur, 'he refused to allow me to go to any of the social functions that he attended. His excuse was that my upbringing and deportment were not suitably satisfactory for a Mytikas. My younger brother Eros, on the other hand, had been raised in the bosom of high society and attended all the best schools.'

'How cruel of him,' Pandora breathed, a sudden surge of feeling clutching at her chest as she saw the flash of emotion in Xander's face. The memory hurt him, she realised. But just as quickly as he had shown his vulnerability he shut it down, lifting his glass of wine to his lips and looking away from her.

'Zeus was a cruel man. You should know this more than anyone.' He shrugged. 'I'm not trying to seek sympathy, Pandora. I'm just…'

He paused, his jaw ticcing. 'I'm trying to tell you I understand what this must feel like to you. That it can be strange, entering this world. I won't lie to you and say that it will all be smooth sailing. It can be an unforgiving place for those who were not born into it.'

'I have more than my fair share of experience of not fitting in,' she admitted, grateful for this moment of honesty between them. 'It would have been better for you to have a proper society bride in all this, but once I commit to something I follow it through, however challenging it turns out to be.' She meant the words, she realised with a little shock. Now that she was past the point of return on their bargain, she felt herself wanting not only to follow through but to do it well. To prove to herself that she *could* play this role, even if it was only for one year.

'I admire that.'

Their eyes met for a long moment, before she quickly glanced back down to her champagne glass. The moment was suddenly too intimate, too much for her to process.

She closed her eyes, inhaling a deep breath for five seconds and releasing it slowly with control. When she opened her eyes again Xander was right there, taking the glass from her hands and placing it gently on the table.

The jet's conditioned air was cool on her bare skin and she stood up, grabbing her wrap from where she'd abandoned it near the entry door. The space was sumptuous and sleek, decorated in white and silver with deep red marble-effect accents. It was one of the benefits of living in the clouds, she mused to herself as she took her time inspecting the fresh roses and hydrangeas that she'd picked in Xander's rooftop garden for her makeshift bouquet.

The rooftop garden of Xander's office where they'd been married was quite possibly the most beautiful place she had ever seen in New York. But that should not be a surprise as she knew that he seemed to gravitate towards rare and expensive items like his bespoke suits and the collector's edition sports car he drove. He was certainly an appreciator of perfection.

She wondered what she looked like through his eyes. Did he notice her autistic traits? She knew that there was no need to inform anyone about the fact that she was on the autism spectrum. But for some reason, she'd been ready to lay it all out for him that morning in his office...before she had got distracted by kissing him, of course.

Perhaps she had wanted to test him. Or maybe that small, scared part of her had hoped that if he knew, he might have called the whole thing off. Either way, they both knew that she was only a temporary fixture here. She would never truly fit into Xander Mytikas's perfect world on a permanent basis. She faltered a little at the thought, her steps scuffing slightly on the carpeted aisle between the jet's plush seats.

A firm hand cupped her elbow, fingers sliding around her skin like a band of steel. Holding her balance upright and preventing her from entering into an embarrassing tumble backwards as she sat down in her seat.

'I'm sorry, I get a little clumsier if I'm distracted.'

'That happens a lot around me, I've noticed.' He raised one brow, his lips quirking with wry amusement. 'Do I distract you?'

Pandora stiffened. Of course he couldn't know the impact that such a benign statement would have on her. But then again, he had no idea of the extent of her difficulties.

'I'm sure you've noticed many of my quirks by now.' She took a deep breath. 'It's because I'm autistic. If you have something you'd like to ask me about that, go ahead.' It was only once the words had left her mouth that she heard the hostility in them, and the defensiveness she was so used to holding at bay.

He raised a brow at her tone. 'If you're asking

if I intend to interrogate you about the nuances of the autism spectrum, I thought I might save that for our wedding night.'

His words entered her mind on a jumble, and for a moment she couldn't focus on anything other than *wedding night* and the shockingly intimate picture that it evoked in her mind's eye. She coughed, realising he was probably being sarcastic, but she still needed to take a few hearty gulps of ice water in an effort to cool her deviant mind. It didn't work.

'Not that this is actually our wedding night in any real sense…' He tailed off, looking mildly concerned when she stood up again rather suddenly.

'You can, if you want. Interrogate me, I mean.' She moved away from him, inspecting some of the delightful desserts that had been laid out on a tray at the bar. A bar on a plane…this place was utterly ridiculous and she was pretty sure she'd never enjoy normal travel ever again.

'I wasn't actually planning to interrogate you,' he assured her with a frown. 'You haven't mentioned it to me before today, for your own good reasons, I'm sure, and despite my recent harsh demands…'

He stood up too, his powerful form only taking two strides before he was leaning against the counter beside her. She stiffened, inhaling the beguiling scent of him and feeling it stir up her senses ever more. Damn him. For a moment she almost wished he would say something inappropriate, like insist that she look at him, just so she could have an excuse to be as worked up as she currently felt.

'I do tend to respect people's boundaries, normally,' he said gently. 'These past twenty-four hours or so haven't exactly been business as usual for either of us.'

'I don't feel the need to disclose my diagnosis with everyone I meet, but that doesn't mean I avoid the topic either,' she explained stiltedly. 'As my husband, I assumed you might need to know, in case it ever came up.'

She felt a familiar tic in her jaw as she spoke, her body reacting to the uncomfortable conversation. She waited, counting her own breaths as Xander seemed to measure his own words before responding.

'Do I need to know all the details, if you'd rather keep them private?' he asked. 'I mean, do you need me to know them in order for me to understand you better?'

The air around them went too quiet, and she swore that she could feel a hum begin in her chest and move upwards into her throat. The surge of emotion choked her, somewhere between her chin and her collarbone. She swallowed hard, grateful that she was facing away from him so that he wouldn't see just how deeply his words had affected her.

No one had ever asked her that before…

She had always tried not to let her difference define her, but the truth was it did. It was a part of her identity, one that she had worked hard to understand and accept with love. The only problem was that other people didn't always see it that way. The idea that he was *asking* if she wanted him to understand her better…she had never even considered it.

'I didn't mean to sound flippant.' He moved closer, his face coming into view by her side. 'I simply mean that it's not a requirement that you tell me everything. This marriage will only work if we each maintain our personal boundaries.'

Pandora simply nodded and turned her back to continue making her tea, knowing that his words held a thinly veiled warning. The trouble was, she had always had difficulty with impulse control. And right now, Xander was a shiny red button, that read *do not press*.

So, of course, she immediately wanted to find out what would happen if she did, how far she could push him, even as the thought of it scared her to her core. It made no sense and yet it made her chest prickle with a kind of terrible excitement. The kind of excitement you only felt when you knew you were skirting the edge of danger. 'Chaos personified', he had once called her during a particularly frustrating meeting… He had no idea.

He moved past her, his suit trousers brushing against the voluminous skirt of her dress. Breath entered her lungs with such sharpness it almost hurt.

But as he paused, his eyes questioning hers silently before he moved back towards his seat, she realised with sudden clarity that she no longer just had a crush on her boss…this man was now her husband, and if she wasn't very, very careful she could easily find herself well out of her depth.

Xander lay back in the jet's recliner chair, sleep still evading him. The memory of that look on Pandora's face when he had moved in to kiss her cheek at their wedding… He definitely hadn't imagined the heat in those silver depths. But this was a woman he needed to keep at arm's length. He had known that from the very first moment he'd laid eyes on her and she'd smiled so warmly at him.

Of course, he'd soon understood that was pretty much how Pandora Quinn treated everybody that she worked with. Her sunny chaotic personality in the office was notorious. As was her seeming naivety, which he had seen in action a few times when he'd noticed people trying to take advantage of her kindness.

He'd put an end to that rather quickly, making his displeasure known to them.

Xander realised for the first time that he had not truly considered how a woman might feel at being a replacement bride. For there was no denying that was what she was.

He thought of the very first night that he'd seen Pandora Quinn, two months before he came to work in New York. That night she had simply been a nameless blonde who had caught his eye at the annual Mytikas Charity Gala, a pompous grand affair that Zeus had thrown every year under the guise of raising money for Greek orphans, when really it was simply another opportunity that he'd used to conduct his own nefarious dealings.

Her eyes had been what had drawn him first, filled with such tension. He had never been the kind of man attracted to a damsel in distress, but he had watched as she'd struggled to disengage from conversing with one of the wealthy businessmen in attendance, backing slowly towards one of the exit doors that led to the foyer. But the other man hadn't seemed to get the memo, and so after observing closely for a couple more minutes and feeling his own blood pressure rise, Xander had intervened.

He couldn't even remember what he had said, only that within a few moments he had extracted her from the situation and she had begged him to get her out of there. He had taken her outside, knowing the old library well considering he himself often ducked out of such events. Every year.

He'd led her to one of the smaller libraries, meaning to quickly deposit her there and head back to the party himself. But just as he had moved to leave he had felt her hand on his elbow and she had offered the words that had probably sealed their fate.

'You could always just hide here too.'

And he had. Before he'd realised it, an hour had passed and a single glance out at the corridor showed a crowd of guests had begun to disperse, some of them heading directly for them. His mystery blonde had excused herself to go to the bathroom and he had been commandeered by his father to break up a spat that had broken out between Arista and one of their board members.

When he had returned to find her, she had gone.

Disappeared as though she had never existed in the first place. And when he had asked his father if he knew the young blonde woman, Zeus had been strangely tight-lipped. Except for a malicious gleam, which Xander in retrospect should have been wary of.

Monday morning had dawned, and he had walked into his office to say goodbye before flying back to Europe, only to find his father waiting, his brand-new executive assistant, Pandora Quinn, in tow.

It had been wrong of him not to acknowledge in any way that they had already met, but rage and previous experience of people who'd tried to take advantage of knowing him had clouded his own judgement. Neither of them had ever once referenced that first night, not even when Zeus had announced his forced hiatus eight weeks later, recalling Xander from Europe, and they had been suddenly forced to work side by side.

He'd always wondered about the swiftness of her hiring. Now, after her attempts to retrieve something from the safe, something that Zeus had supposedly 'promised' her, he knew that something more had been going on behind her sudden employment with his father... He remembered her indignant claim that she was not a criminal, despite being caught red-handed—was it possible that Pandora had been just as much a victim of Zeus's machinations as he was?

And now, in the face of her questionable deceit, was it possible that he had decided to punish her in the same fashion as his father had always punished him? The thought made him absolutely sick to his stomach. His father had been cruel, he had played with people's emotions and used what they wanted against them in order to maintain control.

Xander never did that. But he had demanded that she become his wife, for goodness' sake. He had demanded she play the part of the temporary society bride, not even bothering to ask how that might impact her for the duration. In his mind, she had owed him the service. For him, she had got in the way of what he wanted and so she had to pay the price.

He was no better than Zeus. Perhaps, he was even worse. That thought was enough to keep him awake, stomach roiling and head pounding as the jet moved across the Pacific and into darkness once more.

Finally, having not had a wink of sleep, he got up to find her. He hovered outside the door of the main cabin, where she'd gone to rest, needing to clarify those points with her. To know if his suspicions about Zeus somehow manipulating her were true. But then, as though on cue, a bang sounded from the room within, granting him due cause to open the door and force his way inside, where the bed, though unmade, was completely empty.

Shock reverberated through him, filling him

with adrenaline as he pushed his way further into the room, eyes scanning the perimeter. She had definitely come in here earlier. He had heard the door snap shut behind her.

He was just about to burst back into the main cabin and search every corner, when a small rustling sound caught his attention. The large double bed took up most of the cabin, but for small spaces on either side. The far side of the bed was where the noise had come from.

Xander climbed across the bed, peering down to where the Egyptian cotton duvet had apparently fallen to the floor. He lifted one corner and smelled the scent of roses.

Pandora lay in a foetal position, seemingly rolled up in the duvet like a delicate burrito of sorts.

Her eyes opened, her entire body snapping to attention with a speed that led him to believe that she hadn't been sleeping.

'What are you doing in here?' she asked. 'Have we landed?'

'I think a better question is what are you doing down there?' He resisted the urge to assist her as she pulled herself awkwardly upwards from the small space. 'This is a ten-thousand-dollar bed and you're sleeping on the floor.'

'I couldn't sleep.' She stared at the huge bed,

clearly embarrassed. 'I move around a lot. It felt too open.'

He stared down at her, seeing the dark bruises under her eyes. There were still seven hours before they landed in Osaka, but at this rate they'd both be hallucinating from sleep deprivation. He helped her up from the small space, easing her shoulders back until she was sitting on the side of the bed.

'Okay, the way I see this we could both be stubborn and suffer, or we could just join forces here.' He gestured to the empty bed, then lifted a hand to silence her immediate interruption. 'Think about it, Quinn—I'll fill up the empty space and you will stop banging around my jet waking me up.'

'Xander, honestly, I'm used to finding new ways to cope.'

'You don't need to cope. You need to sleep.'

She blinked up at him, whatever words she'd been about to say wiped out by a sudden gigantic yawn. He felt the urge to follow suit, his eyes feeling heavy almost as though he were drunk. Without thinking, he walked to the other side of the bed and sat down, removing his shoes and lying down to stretch out on the soft white sheets. As expected, the pillows were heaven and he let out a deep growl of appreciation.

'Lie down. Let's just try sleeping together.' He

paused, inwardly cursing his own foolish choice of words. 'Sleep *beside* one another, I mean.'

She was already lowering herself to the pillow on the opposite side of the bed, her lips pursed as she stiffened. 'Sorry, I'm not good at accepting help.'

That simple admission cut through him, unravelling an anger within him towards whoever in her past had made her close up this way. 'Lie quietly with me for five minutes and if it doesn't work, we'll resort to alcohol.'

'Okay,' she breathed, eyes threatening to close even as she whispered, 'This probably won't work, Xander.'

'Why is that?' he whispered back, simultaneously amused and curious.

'You're too good-looking,' she mumbled, sighing. 'And you kissed me.'

He stilled, suddenly realising his own mistake as she relaxed fully into sleep and lazily slid one of her legs outwards, anchoring it under his. The sigh she let out was glorious torture as she drifted into what was most certainly a sound sleep. And he knew he was definitely not going to be getting any rest himself.

CHAPTER SEVEN

PANDORA AWOKE GROGGY and disorientated after what had possibly been the most peaceful few hours' sleep of her life, only to find herself alone in a strange bedroom with Xander's scent all over her skin. A quick peek through the doorway showed him reclined and sleeping peacefully on one of the large seats in the main cabin.

She had practically used him as a teddy bear, she thought with a grimace. A six-foot-four solidly muscled teddy bear who emanated a mind-fogging cloud of pure sex.

She exited the bedroom to her own chair in the cabin and readjusted herself in her seat, feeling a familiar discomfort creep over her body. Her clothes felt too tight, her shoes pinched and every tiny sound in the plane seemed to build together, forming an orchestra of minute micro irritations.

Her sensory system was overloaded and every sound and movement around her had all the impact of a pane of glass shattering against her skin.

New places and exciting experiences were something she absolutely adored but still had to work extra hard to participate in. That kind of mental exertion usually took a huge toll on her energy levels, even if she'd managed a full night's sleep. This was something that she had figured out quite quickly as a child when she'd spent most of her time shouldering the burden of her parents' busy travel and events schedules. She had unconsciously developed ways of hiding her own discomfort, coping silently through the pain so as not to be an extra burden.

But this wasn't the same, she reminded herself. Here with Xander, she was consciously stepping into the temporary role of the billionaire's bride with her eyes wide open. She wasn't denying herself or breaking that silent vow she'd made with herself all those months ago. This was just business.

Xander awoke just as the pilot announced their descent just before midnight in Osaka.

The interior of the sleek car that came to pick them up on the tarmac bore the Tanaka emblem, confirming Pandora's suspicions, but she nevertheless relished the opportunity to talk briefly to the chauffeur in his own language. Japanese had been the fourth language she'd learned but it was one of her favourites. Still, the effort of focusing on the flow of conversation was far more diffi-

cult than usual and when they finally slid into
the passenger area, she almost groaned with relief. The modern car was dark and soothing and
smelled of expensive leather. But most of all, it
was incredibly quiet thanks to the modern engine, and for once she was immensely grateful
for her husband's stony silence as he tapped away
on the screen on his lap.

She watched as the city lights came into view
and Xander asked the driver to take the scenic
route, though his eyes didn't venture up to take
it in himself. Pandora drank in the luminescent
skyscrapers and impossibly bright displays that
made up the modern city at night. Go-karts with
colourful cartoon characters whizzed past them
as they made their way along, tourists and locals
lining the streets. Midnight in Osaka was evidently prime time for fun. She took in the chic
mannequins lining the shopfronts in the fashion district, noting with interest that this seemed
like a city of style. She looked down at her own
simple black jeans and teal T-shirt combination
and cringed.

Her eyes growing tired again, she turned in her
seat slightly, allowing herself a fleeting glance
upwards, and was rewarded with the sleek profile of Xander's patrician nose and razor-sharp
jawline. His long, lean frame took up most of
his side of the car, a scant few inches separating

their thighs from touching. He was distracted, catching up on whatever email correspondence he'd missed out on during his sleep. As his EA, her job would normally have been to prioritise those emails for him. Running a corporation with multiple global time zones was no joke, as she'd found out pretty quickly.

It wasn't that she was lamenting the loss of working with Xander himself, but she had genuinely enjoyed her job. It had been the longest position she'd held, other than working with her mother, and she had just started to feel as if she was settling in. She'd had a reputation as a problem solver, despite her truly terrible organisational skills. She had felt a sense of purpose in her work. She had even begun to feel as if she was good at it, well, good at the translation side of things anyway.

But Xander had told her he'd already hired her replacement, so evidently she wasn't as necessary or valuable to Mytikas Holdings as she might have liked to imagine. What exactly was she expected to do while they were here, if Xander was going to work?

Of course, he chose that moment to look up, capturing her with his icy gaze.

'Problem?' he asked normally enough, but in his deep baritone the word jolted her sensitive nerves and she tensed a little, frozen like a deer in the headlights.

'No, no problem,' she said quickly, lowering her gaze as she fidgeted in her seat.

She had hoped her obvious rebuttal would be enough to close down the interaction and take them back to the pleasant silence that had engulfed them before, but in her peripheral vision she'd seen him place his screen face down on the seat, his gaze still pointedly in her direction.

'You seemed deep in thought.'

'I'm always deep in thought.' She looked up at him briefly, forcing a tight smile to her lips and hoping he didn't see through it. Of course, Xander Mytikas saw everything, a fact she should well know by now.

The silence was back again, only this was not the comfortable one that usually lay between them. This one was filled with a strange tension. When the car finally came to a stop in the wealthy upscale district of Umeda, he exited the car first and offered her his hand, escorting her out into the warm midnight air. Even for early October, the city was still far from the frigid New York autumnal air they had left. But Pandora shivered and stared up at the giant skyscraper where Xander had explained he owned a number of luxury apartments. The interior of the building was rather cold and disappointing, nothing at all like the traditional Japanese décor she'd been expecting.

A doorman escorted them up to the fortieth floor, where Pandora found her bags had already been delivered and unpacked. A light meal sat waiting for them in a modern dining area that boasted a spectacular view of the city lights. The sea of sparkling colours was mesmerising, demanding her full attention. So much so that she didn't hear Xander leave the room until she heard the unmistakeable sound of the shower running.

She was still painfully jet-lagged and disorientated but feeling a mad urge to go and explore the wild urban jungle. This was what she'd promised herself, wasn't it? When she'd accepted Zeus's deal and moved to Manhattan, she'd promised herself more adventures. Surely a billionaire's convenient wife would still be allowed to have fun? Tomorrow, she'd begin her bravery, she assured herself.

The sound of running water came from the larger of the two bedrooms in the sprawling luxury unit, each wall more sleek and polished than the next. She entered the smaller bedroom, frowning to find her things weren't put away in the closets there. They must be in the other room. The water was still running but no way was she risking traipsing into Xander's room to retrieve her things. She had already practically wrapped herself around him on the plane, the last thing she needed was for him to have more reasons to be suspicious of her.

Kicking off her shoes and jeans, Pandora flopped back in the centre of the large four-poster bed in just her T-shirt and underwear and wondered why on earth she had agreed to any of this. It was one thing to find herself married to her boss in twenty-four hours, but it was entirely another to have found herself sharing a bed with him in the sky. Was that something to do with the mile-high club?

The sound of the shower running elicited all kinds of visions in her mind of expensive soap being lathered upon toned muscles and the scent of lemon verbena in the air. There would be steam, she imagined. So much steam and heat and a teasing expanse of slick, freshly scrubbed olive-toned skin...

A door in her own room opened suddenly, making her jump. There must be connecting doorways between the bathroom and both bedrooms, and he'd opened the wrong one. Xander strode out on a cloud of steam, his broad shoulders seeming to fill the doorway.

The towel he had wrapped around his hips was slung so low she gulped. She knew what his workout regimen was like; she had often commented on the predictability of his schedule after all. And yet seeing the deliciously sculpted re-sults of that daily routine was another matter en-tirely. The definition of his pectorals and the lean dips in his hips, the bulging muscles of his thighs, well, the part of his thighs that she could see. It was too much and yet somehow not enough. She licked her lower lip, feeling suddenly parched.

Good grief, he was staring at her and she sud-denly remembered that she was sprawled out on her bed in her underwear. Letting out a very un-ladylike squeak of dismay, she pulled a pillow down into her lap, not that he would be interested much, she told herself. Perhaps he would simply ignore her entirely and pretend she didn't exist. That, she could deal with.

She inhaled a deep breath, letting it hiss out slowly between her teeth as she forced herself to look him in the eye.

Xander Mytikas was trying his very best not to laugh at her.

Good God, she was an absolute train wreck. And instead of answering with some clever quip that made her seem sophisticated or, better yet, made him completely doubt his sexual prowess, Pandora did the worst possible thing.

She threw the pillow at him.

She didn't know why she did it, she only knew that she needed to defuse the awful ten-sion threatening to burn her abdominal muscles to cinders. It seemed to arc across the bedroom in slow motion in a direct line for his smirking face. He caught it before it even came close to hitting him, his still-wet muscles glistening as he flexed. Of course, the infuriating man had the reflexes of a cat as well as the body of a god.

'Sorry.' She sat up against the headboard. 'I didn't mean to…'

'You didn't mean to pick up a pillow and deliberately aim it at my face?' One dark brow was raised in her direction. 'You know, if we were still in the office, this *could* be classed as bullying.'

'You were mocking my discomfort. I acted in self-defence.' She sniffed, pressing a hand against her stomach to tamp down that annoying heat once again.

'Tell me, Pandora…what exactly was making you so uncomfortable?'

His question was seemingly innocent, but… was she imagining it or had his voice lowered slightly? He still stood a few feet from the bed, patiently waiting for her answer.

'You know what you look like, Xander. I'm not going to inflate your monstrous male ego any further.'

'Monstrous.' That damned smirk was widening. 'That's a very unattractive word to use. I'm wounded. And yet…my looks have never made

you act this way in the past. What changed, I wonder?'

'This, obviously.' She gestured vaguely in the direction of his naked chest where the red pillow was fast devolving into a soggy mess. Goodness, she knew the feeling.

'Which part, exactly?' He made a show of looking confused, glancing downwards. 'Just so I know what to keep out of your sight for future reference.'

Against her will, her eyes followed, raking over his perfect pectorals and downwards to where a treasure trail of trimmed hair led to… She inhaled sharply, looking up to find his eyes on her, watching her without a single trace of the humour that was there before. In fact, he looked almost…angry. Which was utterly ridiculous, because he was the one who'd started this whole thing, not her.

After a moment he cleared his throat. 'You're in the wrong bed.' And with that he strode from the room, leaving all the connecting doors open behind him.

She lay still, listening to the sounds of him moving around his bedroom, no doubt trying to find something to cover up his nudity so that his awkward little bride would stop ogling him like some kind of sex-starved nymphomaniac.

Fighting the urge to groan her sheer mortifi-

cation into her pillow, she lay back and stared at
the silky ivory canopy above the bed.

Perhaps if they had been a true married couple
this would be the kind of thing that they would
laugh about. But they were not truly married, he
was not truly her husband and he most definitely
was not hers to stare at like a piece of cake in a
shop window.

She felt the bed dip and suddenly she was no
longer alone under the canopy.

'What are you doing?' She sat up bolt straight.

'I'm a man of my word,' he said simply, lying
back on the pillows. 'If you won't come into the
other room, I'll sleep with you in here.'

It was a ridiculously large bed, big enough for
them to both spread out and still be in no danger
of touching. And yet, she swore the entire room
heated up by a few degrees, as though her skin
could sense him nearby.

'Are you comfortable?' he asked, his voice
floating across the bed. 'Do you need me to move
closer so you can sleep?'

She made a prim noise of assent as she continued to ensure that her body remained still and out
of accidental touching range. The bed moved as
she felt a large weight dip to her left. She didn't
dare to look.

'That's enough, thanks.' She practically

breathed the words. Praying he didn't choose this time to ask any more questions.

She didn't know how long she lay stiff, her mind racing. It was like this sometimes, during times of change. As if she had drunk a vat of caffeine and seven different streams of consciousness were battling for prime position in the forefront of her mind's eye. Couple that with sharing a close space with Xander's delicious scent and, well… She closed her eyes in frustration rather than hope, knowing she would not get any more sleep that night.

She could sense it, the moment his breathing deepened and sleep claimed him. A quick glance over her shoulder confirmed it, as his long eyelashes lay completely still at the top of his cheeks. It seemed there was nothing unattractive about him, as was evidenced by his strong patrician profile in the moonlight as Pandora tried and failed to drift off to sleep. She hadn't meant to stare at him, while she was tossing and turning, but she could only ever fall asleep on her left side, so therefore the only thing in her vision was his face.

He had such a touchable face.

She closed her eyes at the thought, feeling the urge rise within her to follow through on it, to reach out and touch his strong jaw, his sharply jutting cheekbones. This had always been a problem for her, going right back to her childhood. Much to the horror of her parents, their unruly daughter had once insisted on touching every single dish at a celebration buffet just to see what they all felt like.

Impulsivity, her father would check off on his mental list. Father seemed to be the only one who noticed all her quirks and kept a log of her progress over the years. Mother was so busy with her career that she'd had no choice but to delegate the management of the daughter who'd needed so much extra time to her husband.

But when her brother had come along, with his inability to speak at all and his very obvious physical stimming and his wild mood swings… Well, no one had been able to ignore that. She had been twelve the first time she'd heard the word *autism* spoken, but it had not been in relation to herself. Her brother, Odin, had been three then, just started in preschool. Her own diagnosis had come more than a year later, and pretty soon family life had devolved into a series of appointments and progress charts.

Now, the only tracking of her own progress she did was trying to shave down her time on the treadmill. Running centred her mind and helped with her coordination. It was the only part of the intense therapies she'd endured that she elected to continue as an adult.

Regular movement was essential to her well-being, as was nurturing her other innate needs, even if they weren't exactly considered to be normal.

Whatever *normal* was supposed to be.

As her thoughts wandered, she became aware of a heavy weight sliding over her thigh. But rather than feeling threatened, she felt grounded and leaned into his touch, glorying when he covered her leg with his own completely.

She opened one eye, her breathing slow and deliberate and her heartbeat thundering in her ears. His face was still completely relaxed in sleep. But as she watched him, he moved again, a low moan escaping his lips. Pandora inhaled a deep breath, scandalised by the erotic noise and her own body's instant response to it. She should turn around, she told herself firmly and began to inch backwards, carefully trying to dislodge the heavy weight of his thigh.

Her progress was stopped by a firm male arm sliding around her waist.

'Stop moving, Quinn.'

The low rumble of his voice murmured against her hair, startling her. He was clearly still asleep, but Pandora instantly obeyed the command. She focused on steadying her own erratic breathing, inhaling the delicious scent of his lemon verbena soap. To her surprise, every muscle in her body began to relax, almost as though she were melting. She fought the urge not to groan in sheer delight.

She highly doubted that her convenient husband would be pleased to wake up and find himself wound around her so closely. She would just wait another couple of minutes until she was sure he was asleep, and then she would move him.

That was the last thought she had before sleep claimed her.

The morning was already well advanced outside the bedroom window when Xander felt his body snap to attention. Someone had been…moaning? He stilled, listening to the sound of heavy breathing for a long moment before he realised that the sound had come from his own chest.

He had been dreaming. He never dreamed. It had been so detailed, so intense… A fine sheen of sweat beaded his brow and his chest barrelled out with his still-fast breaths. He felt as if he'd just finished completing the erotic acts that had played out in his subconscious mind. He had taken Pandora gently at first, and then much harder until they were both loud and frantic with pleasure. The memory of it was enough to have all the blood in his body immediately rushing south.

Soft curves nestled firmly against his front from sternum to knee.

But worse, his erection was now pressed between the indentation of his new wife's deliciously toned buttocks.

He supposed waking up nestled into a soft, vanilla-scented female body without any chance of release would do that to a man. Even a female he didn't fully trust. Or did he?

Even if he was still suspicious of her behaviour in the safe, he was not so arrogant as to believe that she would deliberately engineer a situation that had them sharing a bed. He had seen her on the plane; she'd been vulnerable. And no matter how out of control his libido seemed to be around her soft curves, he would not be taking advantage of his new wife by seducing her.

He carefully backed away, managing to get off the bed and into the bathroom without waking her.

But even after showering vigorously, he still swore he could feel the heat of her against him.

She didn't wear the usual heavy exotic brands of perfume of the women he'd dated in the past. Her scent was lighter, almost like a breeze in a summer garden. He remembered her face as she had watched him emerge from the bathroom. If he had any doubts as to her level of sexual experience before, her stunned reaction had spoken volumes.

Pandora Quinn was not often in the presence of semi-nude men, he would bet his life on it.

Not that he had any business ruminating over her relationship history. But she was his wife for the next year, so didn't he deserve to know that he would not be made to look a fool in public from any romantic skeletons in her closet?

His own inability to remember whether or not he'd mentioned these terms to her suddenly seemed vitally important and took up much of his attention on the short drive to the Osaka head-quarters of the Tanaka Corporation for his lunch-time meeting. The building had an older feel to it than the others on the streets of the upscale fi-nancial district, which was fitting considering the Tanaka family had been among the first families to set up their investment firms in Japan.

The Tanaka Corporation owned the entire building including an impressive top-floor jun-gle made of glass and wood, filled with exotic plants and solar lighting; it truly was the jewel of the city. He felt the familiar pull of longing, the urge to obtain it. This particular building was the main draw for him in buying them out. He had grand plans for what he would do with it, but first, he needed to clinch the final part of this deal in person.

The investors were already seated at the long table when he entered, and he felt the awareness of dozens of curious eyes upon him as he strode into the room. Ran Tanaka, oldest daughter of the family and a powerful businesswoman in her own right, had been their key contact over the past weeks as they'd tried to broker the extremely time-sensitive and urgent acquisition. Tanaka Corporation was sinking and needed a silent buyout fast in order to keep their historic image intact. It was a deal that Xander urgently needed to make if he wanted to be able to take a foothold in Japan, after decades of bad press and disrespectful moves by Zeus had previously shut them out.

He had expected a difficult summit meeting as both sides finalised the last of their demands, but what he hadn't expected was the atmosphere of sheer disdain when he arrived at the meeting alone, without his highly regarded EA in tow. It seemed that Pandora was a firm favourite, especially with Ran. The other woman's face noticeably dropped when Xander revealed their hasty nuptials and Pandora's sudden resignation from the office.

'She's far too talented to be cooped up in the tea rooms all day like a tourist, Xander. She was at the very heart of this deal and you've left her out.' The other woman sighed, then sat up straight as there was a hubbub out in the hallway.

A man burst into the room, his face wrin-

kled and worn, showing his ancient years. Hari
Tanaka, the family's patriarch and former CEO,
burst into the room, his gaze immediately landing on Xander, before launching into a speech
that Xander was clueless to interpret. Maybe he
should have swallowed his pride and his doubts,
and brought Pandora with him regardless of what
she'd been doing in Zeus's safe?

'He wants to know why you fired Pandora,'
Ran said softly under her breath. 'He hears everything. Good grief, Xander, you do realise that
girl was pretty much the only thing keeping this
deal afloat.'

'Tell him that as the acting CEO of Mytikas
Holdings, I am here to finalise the deal personally.' He pasted on a serene smile, only dropping
it when everyone at the table remained stubbornly silent as Hari kept talking.

'He says that he cannot trust a man who loses
his employees so easily and treats his wife so
disrespectfully by leaving her alone on her honeymoon instead of bringing her.' Ran sat back in
her chair, pinching the bridge of her nose. 'Especially considering the crimes we already hold
your father accountable for. He too was well
known for his disregard of honour and tradition.'

Xander stood up, feeling the tension within
him soar. 'I am not my father.'

'That remains to be seen.' The old man stood

up, switching into perfect English. A bad sign. 'We have received two other offers, lower than yours but from more reputable companies. Either of those would be preferable to doing business with you. We're done here.'

When Xander finally returned to the apartment after walking the streets for several hours deep in thought, Pandora was out on the balcony with her back to him, the evening light turning her hair into a halo around her shoulders. He made sure to clear his throat before sliding the door open, feeling a strange little twist in his abdomen when she turned. But she didn't smile at him in her usual sunny way; in fact, one look at the downset of her mouth and he knew that something was very wrong.

'How did the meeting go?' she asked flatly.

'Terribly, but why do I have a feeling you already know that?'

She grimaced, looking down at the phone in her hand. 'I just got off the phone with Ran Tanaka.'

Xander felt his blood pressure rise.

'Why is she calling you?'

She ignored his question, opening up her tablet to what looked like a presentation. He narrowed his gaze. 'Why do you have a copy of today's files? They're highly confidential.'

'Ran sent them over to me after you stormed out of their building in a rage.'

Xander scowled. 'Miss Tanaka should be directing any changes to me, not my wife, who she knows damn well is no longer working for my company.'

CHAPTER EIGHT

'XANDER, I'VE BEEN working on this deal alongside you for months now,' Pandora urged, walking to the opposite side of the balcony. The normally unflappable businessman she knew Xander to be was gone and she hardly recognised the man in his place. 'What was said to make you react this way?'

'Does it matter?' he growled. 'The Tanaka family are doing this on purpose to make me walk away from the deal. They've either got a better offer or they're trying to up the bidding.'

'Ran is opposed to her father's position. She still believes in your vision for the merger and called me to ask for my help in…handling you.'

She swore if Xander's brows flew up any further they'd go into orbit.

'*Handling* me? I am the acting CEO of this company.'

'And right now you are acting like a spoilt child.' Pandora placed her hands on her hips.

'Your previous approach in the boardroom will not work here, so if you don't want to lose this deal then you will need to change. Adapt.'

'I cannot believe this! The old man was supposed to have stepped down and left Ran in charge. That was the entire reason for my confidence in this whole—'

'Listen. You can sit here and throw a handsome-billionaire fit over the unfairness of it all, or you can listen to my plan.'

Xander scowled, leaning against the railing of the balcony, said handsome-billionaire jaw gleaming with the impressive beginnings of a silver five o'clock shadow. Pandora gulped, resisting the urge to move closer and run her fingers over that jawline; it looked razor sharp but she'd bet it was still soft to the touch. Realising her thoughts were wandering, she cleared her throat loudly and opened up the files Ran had already talked her through.

'Mr Tanaka has his heart set on the business remaining family-owned, even after the buyout. He's concerned for his employees and his children's futures. Ran believes that if you show him that you are not the lone wolf he has heard about, he will withdraw his objections.'

'He won't care what my family values are. I'm Zeus Mytikas's son and that's all he can see. He's already made up his mind about me.'

'You may share his bloodline, but you and I both know the similarities end there.' She frowned at how quickly he brushed off her words, at how determined he was to keep himself inside this box of his own making. Quaking a little, she stepped in front of the balcony doors, blocking him from retreating. 'Xander, most people see the world through their own selfish lens but you're different. I noticed it from the first moment we met. You have this aloof, self-possessed air and yet you care about every single person who works for you. You can try to deny it but… I've watched you.' She pressed her lips together, continuing when he didn't interrupt.

'You make people feel seen. You made me feel seen. You're on this mission to change all the bad things your father has done but you seem so determined not to look at the good that is already there. We need to show him that we are a team and that Mytikas Holdings also has strong family values. That we value tradition and honour, despite the bad blood that Zeus has stirred up over the last couple of decades.'

'How exactly am I supposed to do that?'

'By using your secret weapon, of course.' Pandora smiled, taking a theatrical curtsy. 'Ran has arranged for us to attend a grand reopening ceremony in Kyoto. It's the Tanaka family's home city and a very traditional event.'

He frowned. 'Appearing at an event won't turn the tables in our favour.'

'Of course not,' she agreed. 'But in the meantime, I'd like to temporarily resume working with you until the deal is done. Together, I think we can do this.'

She waited, holding her breath and worrying she'd overplayed her hand until, shockingly, Xander nodded in agreement. 'We could do with your eyes on it, I agree. I'll have you hired as a freelance translator.'

Freelance. The words rang in her mind all evening like a revelation as they ate take-out sushi side by side in the apartment's dining area and she got up to speed on what she'd missed from the meeting. Happiness filled her up, her mind whirring with the relief of having a problem to unpick once more. She was determined to show the Tanakas the true Xander Mytikas, the one he didn't even seem to know himself.

The following days were a blur of public appearances around Osaka to show their front of perfect coupledom. Late nights were spent hunched over market research and contracts while Xander crunched the numbers. The moment Ran heard that Pandora was now freelancing, she insisted on giving her a temporary office on the top floor of the Tanaka Corporation skyscraper, one that overlooked the city with fabulous views.

Apart from chatting during the select few appearances they made in public, she and Xander didn't speak much to one another, but every night he kept his promise and slept in her bed. Every night she struggled not to reach out and touch him, breaking their fragile truce. And every morning she woke up tangled in his arms for a brief few seconds of bliss before he rolled away.

If he was uncomfortable with their quiet working relationship or intimate nightly routine, he didn't show it. If anything, he seemed to seek her out more and more, arranging a quick private lunch for them in the ground-floor restaurant or asking her to grab some fresh air on one of the airy top-floor terrace areas. As far as the first week of a marriage went, she was pretty sure that theirs was rather unusual. But she felt… happy. Her mind was fulfilled and her nights were peaceful… If only she could get a handle on the rapidly growing feelings she was developing for her husband, everything would be rather perfect.

More than once Ran approached her quietly about hiring her skills for future projects, but Pandora always tactfully steered the conversation away. Xander might have labelled her as a freelance specialist, but she wasn't silly enough to believe that was true. He was just bolstering her ego to make her feel less useless, giving her a title so that his wife wasn't his official employee, but a loophole still existed to allow her to help him close this deal. Yet she discovered she didn't completely want to refuse Ran's tentative job offers and found herself pondering them more than once. But above all there was the small matter of her temporary billionaire husband and the intimidating shadow of the grand society wedding that she was set to return to. Followed by a year of playing the role of his wife…

Ran had assured her that if she wanted to work for the Tanaka Corporation, she could simply make a call. She was fast considering the other woman to be a kind of…friend. Friends had always been few and far between for her, with her childhood filled with travel and her adulthood tucked close under her family's anxiously caring influence. Perhaps a little too caring, she realised, now that she'd had time away from them all. Still, she made sure to send her dad regular photo updates and videos, pointedly leaving out the fact that she was in Japan with her husband.

There was no point in telling them of her hasty marriage just yet, she had already decided. She couldn't lie to the people she loved, yet she wasn't able to tell the truth without revealing all of it… so she'd decided to simply wait it out. She'd have to tell them before the big wedding, otherwise they'd probably see it in the world's media anyway, but she wouldn't expect them to travel so they could attend and, truthfully, she really didn't want them there. Family were for real weddings, not PR stunts, she reminded herself. If she had her father walk her down the aisle, her foolish mind might start actually believing that her fairytale wedding was true.

On their final day of new and improved negotiations, they broke new ground and she felt a buzz of excitement building in their small team. It was late in the evening when a large meeting was held on the top floor between Xander and the board of directors. Pandora wasn't allowed in and so she'd gone back to the apartment to wait, passing the time by sitting on the sofa in the living area with one of the small cross-stitching projects she'd brought with her. She was terrible at it, but it kept her hands busy. Two whole hours had passed by the time Xander strode in, a huge smile on his face.

'We did it,' he announced, looking exhausted and elated and devastatingly handsome. Pandora stood from where she'd been anxiously awaiting the news, relief making her limbs heavy. She wasn't quite sure what the appropriate response was in this case, uncertainty pinning her feet in place as Xander continued to cross the room towards her. Without warning, he lifted her up against his chest and pressed his mouth to hers.

His kiss was hard and hot and filled with so much passion it quite literally took her breath away. But he pulled back almost as quickly as he'd started, a look of complete surprise on his face. 'I didn't mean for that to happen.'

'It's fine,' she said breathlessly, pursing her lips as Xander took a few steps away from her, leaving her body feeling cold.

'*Christos*. I just wanted to thank you.' He attempted to straighten his tie, then lost his patience and pulled it off completely. 'Just when I think I've pulled us back from dangerous territory...'

'It's only a kiss,' she said quietly, leaning against the arm of the sofa.

'We both know it's not. Do you regularly go around kissing people?'

'For me, dating and kissing are unavoidably connected.' She shrugged. 'I don't enjoy one, therefore I don't particularly engage in either.'

'You seemed to enjoy it with me.' Xander frowned, then froze. 'Pandora, are you telling me that I was...forcing myself on you?'

His last words came out slightly strangled and she moved forward quickly, placing a hand in the centre of his chest. 'Absolutely not! I enjoy your kisses, Xander. Probably more than I should.'

His gaze darkened. 'Good.'

'Is it?' she whispered. 'It doesn't feel good. It feels like…torture most of the time. I don't understand why all of a sudden I'm craving something that I've never particularly enjoyed before. Why it would suddenly become appealing with the one person who has made it very clear that he doesn't feel the same.'

She took a step back, feeling vulnerable and unsure of herself. This conversation felt strange, foreign to all their others. But, she supposed, they hadn't been sharing a bed before. As if she had just realised how thoroughly far apart this was from their sensible business arrangement.

'But then again, you're you,' she added, forcing a light laugh from her cold lips. 'We've come to know one another better, so maybe that's the difference. It makes sense that kissing you would feel safe.'

'Safe,' he repeated, the expression on his face dark and unreadable.

'What I mean is…' She scrambled for words. 'We have an agreement between us. There's no emotion involved, no feelings to hurt. It's simple.'

'Simple and safe.' He raised one brow. 'A man wouldn't want to have an ego to uphold around here.'

Xander prowled towards her so that a mere foot lay between them. 'There is nothing simple or safe about the way I feel right now, let me make that clear. If you could see the fantasies I've concocted in my mind…'

The air around them turned thick and heated and she was suddenly thankful for the privacy of their apartment.

'Tell me,' she breathed.

'I want to do more than tell you.' He leaned forward, his hand cupping the underside of her jaw.

Pandora felt the needy heat within her flare to boiling point just from that small contact. This was scandalous, what they were doing. It was wrong. Her eyes were glued to his lips, as though she were transfixed by him. Nothing new there then, she reminded herself. She had felt the inexorable pull towards this man from the moment they'd first met.

But when he was her boss, the line between wrong and right had been very black and white back then, so keeping him at arm's length had been an easy decision.

Xander Mytikas would never have done something so wrong as kiss his plain little assistant. He had been her boss. She had been off-limits.

But that line had been erased and the one that separated them now seemed faded and broken and easily stepped over.

She met his eyes, their cerulean blue filling

her with fizzy warmth, and she almost felt the urge to run. But then he slid an arm around her and held her, her chest pressed so deliciously against his. She took her time staring at the perfect square angles of his jaw and how it met the curve of his ear surrounded by jet-black close-cropped hair liberally speckled with grey, which made him even sexier in her eyes.

All week, she had resisted the urge to run her fingers through his hair. She had despised herself for the impulse that constantly nagged at her awareness whenever he leaned closer over the boardroom table and ran his hand through it as he thought over a particularly difficult point of the negotiation.

She had promised herself that she was strong enough to withstand this pull she felt towards him. She had not banked on the fact that he might feel it towards her too.

Feeling bold, she reached up to the nape of his neck and splayed her fingers through his hair, centimetre by delicious centimetre. It was cool to the touch but smooth as silk, just as she remembered from the last time she'd had her fingers in it. She knew exactly what Xander smelled like. She had been unable to remove the memory of him and his delicious scent from her mind.

And yet it felt right somehow. As if she had always known how it would feel to touch him so intimately. He didn't move to stop her when her other hand moved up the side of his neck to glide along the stubble on his jaw.

'You're stroking me.' He growled huskily, leaning into her touch.

Even though they were alone with no possible reason to be playing their parts, she was plagued with uncertainty. She didn't want that darkness in his eyes to be fake. She wanted that darkness to be hers alone, a result of his powerful attraction to her. An attraction that they both felt.

Feeling foolish, she slowly slid her hands back to rest on his shoulders.

'I wasn't asking you to stop.' Xander took her hands in his and laced her fingers under his own at the back of his neck. He leaned down and pressed his lips against the side of her neck and all thoughts exited her mind.

He murmured something to himself under his breath. His eyes closing as if on a prayer. *'Months.'*

She heard the last word clearly, considering it was growled against her skin like a curse. She felt the vibration of it, of him, as though she'd absorbed it into her. He stilled, breathing heavily, and she could feel the hesitation in him. But he didn't move to back away, if anything he leaned further into the delicious embrace of their bodies.

Pandora felt vulnerable and powerful all at

once with the way Xander's hooded gaze roved over every inch of her body. The top two buttons of her white shirt were undone, her lacy bra peeking out.

'I wanted you from the first moment I laid eyes on you. I'm no better than Zeus.'

She reached up, cupping both hands around his face and feeling the heat of his skin under her fingertips. 'I wanted you too. You're nothing like him, Xander. I'm not your employee any more. I'm your wife.'

The word seemed to light a fire in him and before she could think, he was spreading her legs wide and stepping into the space between them, all the better to undress her...

Xander looked at the dazed expression on Pandora's face and fought the urge to kiss her again, hard and fast. Thinking she might not be ready for that just yet, he settled for bending down and laying a series of hot wet kisses along her naked midriff, tracing a slow path upwards until once again they were on an even eye level.

She was shy without her clothes, not quite meeting his eyes and, *Christos*, if it didn't drive him even more wild. He shrugged off his suit jacket and pulled at the shirt on his back, hearing the pop of a few buttons and the ping as they hit the floor. He didn't care, only pausing long enough to pull it off the rest of the way.

Pandora looked up at him and her eyes traced over his naked chest with slow intensity, her mouth opening to form a little O shape.

'You're so perfect,' she whispered.

Xander paused, looking down to find her eyes filled with such raw desire he thought he might come on the spot. When she touched the rippling muscles on his abdomen, he felt himself shudder. What was she doing to him?

Breathing heavily, he grasped her wandering hand and took it captive, holding it above her head while he finally leaned down to claim her mouth. She gave back as good as she got, holding onto his grip with her other hand and digging her nails in ever so slightly. That hint of pain was enough to tip him over the edge of his control.

His heart pounded in his ears like a war cry, his body demanding the satisfaction of conquering this beautiful, lush bounty. Something pushed against the walls of his subconscious, warning him to hold back, to take a moment, but then her hands moved to grip his waist, pulling him to her, and his body reacted instantly, pulsing forward against her soft core.

Christos.

Too much fabric, his mind roared, and he reached down for the zip of his trousers, fighting the urge to rip them off completely. She joined the frenzy, both of them pulling at his clothing until finally his skin was just as bare as hers. Then he was on her once more, pressing her back onto the sofa and coming over her to lie chest to chest, skin against skin. She opened her mouth to speak but he was already kissing her again, already sinking his free hand into her hair and laying claim to her as their bodies moved against one another with building urgency.

He communicated with each writhing thrust against her thighs that there was no time for words, no time for anything but the primal force beating between them, demanding more. There was no time for anything but this. He had to have her, right here, right now.

He pulled back from the kiss, reaching down to grip the hard, hot length that sat heavy and aching. Biting his lip, he touched his thumb against her molten core, feeling the heat of her coating his skin. Pandora was looking at his erection and, again, the expression of wonder and sheer lust on her face damn near undid him.

'Don't look at me like that. I want this to last.'

'Wait,' she said softly. 'Do you have protection?'

The air seemed to leave his lungs on a single, punishing exhalation and Xander felt his entire world shudder to a grounding stop at that simple question. His mind came crashing back online with stunning focus, taking stock of what they had just been about to do. What Xander had been about to do.

'Xander?'

He heard her voice but he was unable to speak, to look up, for fear of his own reaction. He felt her gentle hands on his chest in a silent question and it was too much, it was all too much right then. He stood up, feeling the cool air hit the raging inferno of his body, and it took all his strength not to just lie back down and continue. With every step he took away from her, his body roared with outrage, his heartbeat pounding in his ears.

The bathroom light felt like a white-hot laser, piercing the haze of lust. He slammed the door behind him, not trusting himself if she decided to follow him.

He felt wild and depraved, holding onto his sanity by the barest thread, and that realisation made his heart race even more. This never happened to him, never. He never lost sight of this part of him, this deep-rooted need he had to be in control all the time. Furious, he slammed his hand down on the marble countertop, feeling pain shoot upwards into his wrist. Ignoring the pain, he slammed it down once more, as though daring his own body to defy him any more than it just had.

He had been ready to plunge himself into her without protection, without any care for the consequences. This arrangement, this marriage…it had got so far under his skin he felt as if someone had reached into his soul and stirred wildly so that every deep, dark part of him had risen to the surface.

It wasn't her fault. And yet, inexplicably, he resented her for it, for being the catalyst that made him feel this way. For a split second he felt the urge to demand that she leave, that he remove the problem at its source, the temptation that was Pandora Quinn. But as he looked at himself in the mirror, imagining the look on her face as he sent her away, he felt himself resist and he knew with absolute certainty that the problem would not disappear just because his wife was no longer within arm's reach.

He wanted to roar his frustration at all of it, every damn thing that bound him and tightened the constraints of being Zeus Mytikas's son. But instead he ran cold water over his sore fist for a few minutes, and then walked back out into the living area.

Pandora sat on the sofa, her body mostly shielded by a red silk throw blanket, but still he ached for her. He pushed the feeling away, pushed everything down until all he felt was cool, hard focus as he reached for his trousers and pulled them on. Pain lanced through his knuckles but he ignored it, his only care focused upon the silent woman studiously avoiding his gaze.

'That can't happen again, Pandora.' He spoke with a remoteness that stunned even him. He saw her flinch ever so slightly and hated himself for it. But instead of responding she simply stood up and grappled silently with the throw, trying not to show any more naked skin than she had to. She walked past him without another look, her chin held high, not stopping until she reached the door of her bedroom. He saw the rise and fall of her shoulders in the moonlight as she inhaled a deep breath, blonde hair shimmering as she shook her head ever so slowly.

'I was wrong.' She looked back over her shoulder. 'You are the furthest thing from safe for me. And there is nothing simple about this attraction between us. I'll try harder to remember that.'

He took a step towards her, needing to explain to her why this was the only option for him. Why this attraction between them could only spell disaster for them both…but Pandora raised her hand to stop him, warning him without words to stay away.

So he did.

Xander didn't come to their bed that night, and she told herself she was relieved.

Pandora sat for a long time, staring out at the bright lights of the cityscape until dawn broke, her thoughts an unbearable vortex of confusion. Confusion over how they had allowed things to go so far so quickly. How she had been so close to making love with a man she had vowed to remain professional with. How she had adored every single minute of it and felt a kind of comfort and connection she had never thought she'd ever feel. And pleasure…so much pleasure.

She felt the uncomfortable clench of chaos whirling within her. There was no work to occupy her mind now. For all the euphoria they'd felt yesterday in winning the contract, she hadn't really processed the fact that, in doing so, she had now completed her temporary freelance contract with Xander. They would travel to Kyoto this evening for the reopening ceremony that the Tanaka family had invited them to, and then tomorrow their 'business trip slash honeymoon' would be over and they would return to New York… Return to whatever came next in this charade of a marriage.

She decided that she would forgo her usual morning run on the treadmill in the building's world-class gym if it meant she could avoid seeing her husband and having to face the fallout of the disaster that was the night before. She needed to get out of this apartment right now. If he woke up and wanted to talk…she knew she would just crumble. Anger fuelled her once more, stiffening her movements as she pulled on her favourite skinny jeans and T-shirt, her feet stumbling slightly in her haste as she stepped into her boots.

He made absolutely no sense. One minute he was hot and heavy, ready to plunge into her, and the next he had practically run from the room. Yes, they had almost forgotten to use protection, but she had remembered in time. There was no risk, no danger. And yet he'd behaved so harshly, returning to the room as though nothing had happened between them, and calmly informed her that there would be no repeat performance.

She closed her eyes, wondering how on earth she was supposed to survive twelve more months of playing Xander's dutiful wife when this first week already had her at the limits of her control.

CHAPTER NINE

IF XANDER HAD been slightly worried at Pandora's ability to perform in light of last night's events, all his concerns had been eased within the first five minutes of their entry into the beautiful gardens where the reopening ceremony was being held.

He looked down at the woman by his side, her delicate porcelain features serene and polite as she conversed easily in Japanese with one of the senior board members of the Tanaka Corporation. His own Japanese was basic and reduced simply to greetings and culturally appropriate words of congratulations or commiserations as he needed in the boardroom. Switching between his native Greek and English was usually enough to stretch his tolerance.

Pandora looked up at him, a slight frown marring her brow when she leaned in ever so slightly, increasing the pressure of her fingers where they rested on his forearm. The movement sent a jolt of electricity through him.

She really needed to stop touching him.

All these small gestures, guiding him, whispering the names of various contacts just before they stood in front of them, offering to get him a drink. She was no more acting like his wife than he was acting like her husband.

The need to confirm to this entire gathering that Pandora was his, in the most primitive sense of the word, consumed him. But he was not the same out-of-control brute he had been the night before so he resisted it. Their marriage was not a tool that he could use to his advantage in the current situation. So why then did he feel such an urge to claim her here, to wipe away the polite façade that she had presented in her perfectly pressed black dress and her tight sensible chignon? Why did anything about her professional conduct all day bother him so badly?

Wasn't it exactly what he had asked for?

It wasn't long before the Tanaka family arrived, finally gracing them with their presence with their usual lack of fanfare, and he was swept into conversation after conversation about the deal they had just made.

'My congratulations again on your excellent choice of bride,' Ran said quietly, drawing him to one side as they watched the festivities.

'I truly believed that you would never find another woman to live up to me.'

'Our time together never leaves my thoughts.' Xander smiled at his own joke, enjoying Ran's sly reference to their single, solitary date a couple of years previously. 'If you ever need my assistance again in that regard, you have my number.'

'You're a married man, behave yourself.' She laughed, smacking at his arm.

A small shuffle sounded from behind them, derailing their conversation while a waiter cleared up someone's spilled drink. Xander took the opportunity to scan the area, finally finding his wife on the path ahead, Hari Tanaka chatting away happily by her side.

'You're happy with her.' Ran smiled. 'I suppose it was a good thing that your brother stole your first bride.'

His gaze snapped up. 'You know about that, then?'

'Everyone knows about that. Their marriage is public knowledge, is it not?'

Xander froze. Eros and Priya had got married? It hadn't been public knowledge last time he'd checked in with his team in New York, but with the time difference, perhaps he'd been off his game. Ran moved away to chat with other guests but Xander stayed put, brooding.

Being made a fool of was the one certain way

to strike through his infamous glacial control. And even now, surrounded by the elite of Japanese society, he felt his boyhood temper flare, the old talk of sibling rivalry drawing him down into the primal core of himself that he had fought for years to suppress.

Pandora's stomach clenched, cold seeping into her bones as she moved quickly away from the private conversation between Xander and Ran that she'd accidentally overheard. She swept through the gardens, her polite smile in place as she inspected the exterior of the shrine, finally coming to a stop on a beautiful red bridge surrounded by tall maple trees. It was quieter here, with most guests mingling nearer to where a fire show was being set up for the evening's entertainment.

Her thoughts swirled darkly as she thought of Xander with the beautiful Tanaka heiress, imagining them together. Why hadn't he told her that they had been an item? Why hadn't Ran told her?

A dark echo of some painful emotion bobbed to the surface within her as she wondered...had they agreed to keep her in the dark together? An uncomfortable emotion made her insides prick up in a strange way, one that in all the months they had known one another she had never felt before. Xander had hurt her.

And for all the giddy excitement she had felt being in this beautiful place, surrounded by such affluence and history, she suddenly felt like the small child at the playground who had absolutely no idea what was going on but was fairly sure that she was the butt of the joke.

It wasn't long before she heard footsteps intruding on her solitude; she turned and found Xander looking painfully handsome.

She tensed, immediately moving a scant few inches away from him. She couldn't think with him touching her. She couldn't breathe.

Suddenly, she felt utterly ridiculous.

'You and Ran seem to be hitting it off nicely,' she said evenly, hoping that her voice held none of the tight emotion that had begun to creep into her chest. They might not have discussed dating other people as part of their marriage agreement, but she was under no illusion that a man like Xander wouldn't be flooded with attention from potential suitors.

Plus, she liked Ran.

'Is that a problem?' He was assessing her face curiously, tension tightening the hand now curved around her elbow.

'Of course not,' she blurted. 'You're a very popular, handsome man in your prime.'

'And you deem that relevant to our current situation, how?'

'Xander, I would simply rather know when you would prefer me to slip away. For appearances' sake, perhaps a higher level of discretion may be needed, but we can always arrange for separate rooms if you're…entertaining someone.'

His eyes widened, a sudden flaring of his nostrils that startled her. Again, his fingers flexed against her bare skin, and her treacherous body responded with an equally sudden shiver of pleasure at the firm contact and she pulled away. She really needed to stop doing that.

Someone touched her elbow unexpectedly and she turned to see Ran smiling by her side. Reflexively she took a step back, her balance shifting unexpectedly. For a long moment, the swathe of beautiful red and orange maples surrounding them seemed to tip and she felt herself falling.

Strong arms caught her and she looked up into Xander's serious gaze. How on earth had he moved so quickly?

Ran's worried voice came from nearby. 'Are you okay?'

Great, Pandora thought wryly, if she hadn't already been the object of their pity before she certainly was now. She could feel the familiar sensation of her social battery beginning to crash, and like Cinderella she suddenly needed to run away, she needed to get out of here before her internal clock struck midnight and she made an even bigger fool of herself than she already had.

But just as she was poised to make some dull excuse and leave her husband to enjoy the rest of the event without her, she felt a familiar warmth settle around her waist. Almost like a dream, she heard Xander make a polite excuse to Ran that they would be leaving early and, just like that, he began propelling her towards the exit.

Pandora followed in a daze until they stood at the bottom of the steep stairs and Xander dipped his head towards her.

'Where is the driver?' He scowled with obvious annoyance. He altered their course, pulling her slowly in his wake. Slowly…he was walking so slowly and carefully, holding her tight as though she might break.

'Stop.' She tripped a little as she removed her arm from his gentle clutches. 'I don't expect you to…mind me. I'm not a child.'

'No, you're not. You're my wife and you're clearly exhausted. Forgive me if I don't want to see you endure a full evening of discomfort when we can easily leave early.'

'But you were enjoying yourself with Ran,' she said, feeling more and more like a petulant child.

Realisation seemed to dawn on him, his lips pressing together. Their driver arrived and Xander herded her into the car, his large body sliding onto the seat beside her. He waited a few moments before he spoke. 'So you overheard my conversation with Ran Tanaka and immediately jumped to the conclusion that I was arranging a…romantic interlude with her.'

'I don't know what you were arranging. It doesn't matter, does it? While I'm quite annoyed with both of you for keeping your personal history a secret, I understand that it's not quite my business.'

Xander turned towards her, one arm sliding along the seat behind her head. 'You are my wife. I'd argue that it's exactly your business.'

Fear and excitement mingled in her blood, making her lose track of her words. Why did he have to affect her like this?

'I helped Ran out, a couple of years back. She needed a handsome date on her arm to make someone else jealous. She's only ever been a friend.' He emphasised the last word softly.

Pandora processed his words slowly, feeling relief and embarrassment war within her chest. 'I've made a mess of tonight, Xander, I'm sorry. Just, please go back and enjoy the rest of the event. I can go back to Osaka alone.'

'You're tired and we are newly-weds, so it's hardly suspicious for us to duck out of an event early.' He sat back in his seat, staring out at the passing lights. 'We're not going back to Osaka. I've arranged for accommodations here.'

Pandora paused, puzzling over the sudden change in plans. 'Why?'

His jaw tightened and he looked strangely self-conscious for a moment. 'Our flight back to New York isn't until tomorrow afternoon and I have no further meetings planned. You said you'd never seen Kyoto. I didn't want you to come all this way and miss out.'

The honest kindness in his words made her throat clench and she barely managed to utter a thank you before her words left her entirely. Why did he have to keep acting so perfectly? The car moved through the ancient city quietly, no more words passing between them. Their driver expertly navigated them through a set of tall wrought-iron gates and wove them uphill, through an avenue of tall maples.

Dusk had fallen, the lights of Kyoto shining in the distance now as they rounded a bend and a beautiful house came into view. It was breathtaking, a mixture of traditional Japanese design and stark modern lines. It was silent and serene as they made their way up the stone steps, the sound of running water coming faintly from nearby.

But once they were inside, alone, Xander turned to her.

'I've been honest with you tonight. I've trusted

you with this deal and yet it seems you're determined not to trust me. In my experience, those who seek out lies are usually the ones hiding something themselves. I think it's time you told me the truth, don't you?'

She felt her anxiety begin to rise and swell once more. He had been honest with her about Ran, even when she'd thought the worst of him. And yet she continued to keep a secret from him that she knew he deserved to know. She trusted him enough to know that he wouldn't punish her in the way that she'd once feared. And yet, she'd still resisted, not wanting to see the look in his eyes when he found out her true deception.

'I know about Titan Corp,' she said on a rush of breath.

CHAPTER TEN

XANDER FROZE, HIS eyes narrowing to slits. 'Explain.'

'I know that you're planning to stage a hostile takeover of Mytikas Holdings once you've accumulated enough shares. I know this because… Zeus told me. He used me…to spy on you and report back.'

'How long?' he gritted out.

'From the moment you arrived in New York he told me that I would be used to get secrets from you. But I promise, I only ever told him the bare minimum I could get away with. He was blackmailing me to work for him.'

'What? How?' Xander looked appalled.

'The first night we met, I was at that gala as a guest with my mother. I had no idea who you were, or who Zeus was to you. You and I never exchanged second names. I'd just had an argument with my mother, I'd overheard her arguing with Zeus and realised that she'd lied about the true nature of our trip to the States. Zeus was holding something over her and was trying to call in a favour, but…she couldn't do whatever he wanted.'

She forced the words past her lips in a rush, knowing that if she stopped, if she so much as looked at him, she would lose her nerve. But still, she could feel his eyes on her.

'Zeus said he had evidence of whatever she'd done, so to get it back, I agreed to work for him. Initially because I had the language skills he urgently needed, and then, after he became ill, he instructed me to spy on you for him. The evidence he had against my mother was what I was looking for in the safe that day of your and Priya's wedding. It was supposed to have been in the file I bargained with you for.'

'Supposed to be? So it wasn't inside?'

Pandora felt her bottom lip quiver, remembering that night when she'd got home and pulled open the file only to find it empty. Not a single scandalous picture or damning email to be found. She'd contemplated calling her mother, but then she would have had to reveal her own bargain with Xander.

'It must have been truly important information, for your mother to sacrifice you into a bargain with a man like Zeus.' His tone was filled with anger. She looked up and was shocked to see barely constrained rage in his eyes.

'My mother refused to allow me to do it, actually. She has always been overprotective of me, my father too. Maybe that was why I defied her orders and insisted that I could handle it.' She could still see the older man towering above her mother, hear him threaten her. 'That night set something off within me, it spurred a need I'd long ignored to take control and prove myself. To show that I was capable of protecting her too.

'You helped me to see that, you know,' she said softly. 'In the midst of it all, before Zeus sought me out once more and made his bargain… I met you. I realised that I wanted more from my life than what I had living in Ireland. You made me realise that I wanted more. I should have known then. It's not normal to have such thoughts about a complete stranger.'

'What kind of thoughts?' he rasped, stepping closer. 'Because they couldn't be any more scandalous than the ones that I've harboured.'

'You…you have?'

'Months,' he whispered. 'Months of remembering that night and wondering what might have happened if we hadn't been interrupted. Months of resisting you and despising him for placing you in front of me. I'm sorry that he used you against me this way. I'm sorry that he deceived you and your mother. Zeus…he knew exactly what he was doing.' The last sentence was a growl, wrought from him.

'Why were you so cold towards me these last four months? Did you believe that I sought you out at the gala deliberately?'

'I was furious with myself. It's no secret that I am the product of my own father's lack of control around his employees. I'd never had a whiff of scandal with anyone who was even remotely subordinate to me. And then there you were, the biggest walking temptation that I'd ever encountered.'

She swallowed the knot of emotion forming in her throat and tried to focus past the pool of longing building within her. With sudden clarity, she knew that if they gave in to the madness again, this time, there would be no stopping either of them.

She wanted to make love with him more than she wanted to breathe. Her body hurt from trying to hold herself together, from trying to deny the raw primal need that filled her every time his body was close. But it was more than just wanting a warm male body against her own; she wanted him. She wanted Xander. And for that reason she took a deep breath and spoke, knowing he might walk away but needing to take that risk.

'I can't pretend that I'm not affected by you,

Xander,' she said, pushing herself to get the words out. 'It's just not the way I'm wired.'

He'd warned her not to expect anything from this marriage. Especially not love. So she needed to keep guarding her heart for all she was worth if she wanted to survive the next twelve months.

'You think that I'm not affected by you?' he asked.

'I have no idea what you think or feel, you are the most infuriating puzzle I have ever encountered and yet... I just keep wanting to push you. To try to unravel that iron-clad control of yours... to see what's underneath that mask you wear for the world. To show what is underneath my own.'

'Is this what you wished I would do?' He pulled her closer. 'You wanted me to take control, to be the demanding boss of your fantasies?'

'Yes,' she breathed, not even caring how crazed she sounded.

'*Christos*... I can barely look at you without wanting to pull you away to the nearest hard surface whether it's a bed or a floor...or a wall.'

'Or a desk?' she suggested.

He groaned, his hands on her face and in her hair, and his mouth sought out hers. She was instinctively sinking into the kiss before she had the sense to pull back.

'This can't be normal, feeling this way. I'm going to combust,' she heard herself say.

'I'm in control here, remember. And, Pandora, this is not normal for me either.'

She felt the hard, hot evidence of his arousal pressing below her belly button, branding her with molten heat. His lips sought the soft flesh beneath her ear, his tongue tracing a slow path along the sensitive lobe that made her shiver. She felt that pull, that delicious fire threatening to burn again and swallow her whole…but she resisted. She needed to get her thoughts out of her head before they took this any further past the invisible line they had already drawn in the sand. Because sexual arousal faded and she had agreed to stay married to him, to stand by his side as his wife for the next year.

Suddenly, what they were doing seemed utterly ridiculous.

She pulled back in the circle of his arms but he kept his hold on her hips, flexing his fingers slightly and sending little bites of sensation through her.

'There's a reason why I don't just sleep with every woman who catches my attention, Pandora.' His voice was like gravel, his eyes dark with intensity. 'I've never even come close to breaking my own rules. Until you…'

She closed her eyes at his words, resisting the warm sensation they evoked deep in her core. A sensation that felt perilously close to hope. That was the one emotion that she had promised herself she would not unleash on their arrangement, no matter what happened between them.

'I've spent four months controlling myself for every moment that I was in your presence.' Xander frowned, running one finger down the centre of her chest, making her shiver. The wide muscular span of his hands came to rest under her ribcage and she felt deliciously caged in, held together by the firm pressure.

'I need to know that you won't regret this in the morning. That if we take this one night for ourselves, we can live with it,' she said. One night would have to be enough. Risking more was to risk a shattered heart.

'One night?' he teased, pulling her closer, fisting one hand through her hair with a touch that managed to be both sensual and deliciously firm all at once. 'Do you deliberately set these limitations, knowing that I am a man who always wants more?'

'I'm serious.' She met his eyes with every ounce of steel she could muster, considering his touch had turned her entire body into a writhing mess. 'It's important to me.'

'One night,' he repeated, his voice as dark as molasses, taunting her resolve and screaming at her to take back the terms. To take as much as she could get of him and his dominant sensuality. To give herself up to him and be damned to the consequences.

But she knew herself too well. She knew how deeply her feelings could run and how quickly that could get a girl like her in trouble. She was too soft for a man like him, she was too trusting. If he gave her an inch of his affection, she would be powerless not to hold out hope for more…and more…

She deserved more than that. Maybe some day she would get it, although she wasn't holding out any hope it would be Xander who gave it to her. But until then, one night with Xander was her own gift to herself. One night of making the bad choice for once in her life, of being selfish and taking what she wanted and dealing with the consequences later. One night…before reality came crashing back down and she remembered all the reasons why this was a terrible idea.

She ran her tongue along her bottom lip and watched as his gaze locked on the movement. She loved how he looked at her, how his gaze tracked her and seemed to home in on every slight shift in her mood. And whatever he saw in her right now seemed to affect him instantly.

Taking her by the hand, he led her up to one of the beautiful master bedrooms, where, sure enough, their luggage had been delivered and put away. She was so busy admiring the view of Kyoto from the terrace windows, she hardly noticed Xander's arms snaking around her waist until he had lifted her and deposited her in the centre of the giant bed. He crawled over her, keeping most of his weight on his forearms, but still she felt the weight of him pressing her down into the soft silk sheets.

But when he gently trailed a finger down her face, she stiffened, her body flinching against the unpleasant sensation.

He paused, and her heart melted a little at the flash of concern in silent question in the furrow between his brows. But how on earth was she supposed to tell him that she needed a firmer touch without it sounding vaguely kinky? She shook her head, determined to just let the moment pass and focus on the delicious sensation of his mouth moving ever closer to the hyper-sensitive skin at the tips of her breasts. But she was forgetting that this wasn't just any man kissing her, this was Xander.

He touched her jaw, again too softly, but there was a hint of steel in his voice that made her shiver. 'If I'm doing something you don't like, tell me.'

She felt the breath whoosh from her lungs at that simple command. And it most definitely was a command.

'I prefer a firm touch,' she admitted.

'Like this?' he asked, his eyes following the path of his fingers as he applied a little more pressure.

Her answer was a low moan and he smiled, his lips filled with pure masculine satisfaction. 'I'm a perfectionist,' he murmured. 'And that trait applies both in and outside the boardroom. I'm going to figure out exactly what you like in bed, Pandora. And then I want to do it over and over again until you can't think any more…just feel.'

'I like…your hand here,' she murmured, shocking herself by placing her own hand on top of his. She closed her eyes, fighting the urge to groan at the pleasure of being touched by him this way. Just his touch… God, she was in so much trouble.

She drowned in the onslaught of pure sensation as Xander kept one hand on her neck and kissed a slow path down into the valley between her breasts. He didn't kiss her breasts so much as he devoured them, slow and steady and with devastating precision. He held her in place as he licked and sucked each throbbing pink tip in turn and she found she was utterly powerless to look away. She felt herself grow even more aroused, imagining watching him do that somewhere else on her needy body. Imagining taking hold of his thick hair and guiding him to where she needed his mouth even more urgently.

She felt herself throb, her body begging for more. Begging for him. But still, she held back. A part of her not fully giving over to the pleasure she was feeling, a part of her still staying on alert just in case she did something wrong.

The thought made her close her eyes suddenly. She would not second-guess herself now. But her body insisted and she was powerless against the urge to switch off.

Xander murmured soothing words against her skin, but the sensations dimmed and her heartbeat slowed a little, as though her subconscious had flipped a dimmer switch. She felt him pause, heard him say her name twice before she remembered to react.

'You with me?' His words were part concern, part rough demand and something about the intensity in his gaze seemed to pull her back from the brink, reminding her that she was not with anyone else. She was with him. Xander.

Almost as though he'd heard her inner struggle, he moved up over her, caging her in with his big muscular body, anchoring her down to the earth once more. She felt her body relax and finally she looked up, her gaze immediately pinned by twin flames of electric blue.

'Just…kiss me,' she whispered and she was relieved when he immediately claimed her mouth, hard and fast.

She breathed into the kiss, into the glorious sensation of having Xander's body on hers, pushing her down. She felt her own body awaken once more, her thighs clamping tightly around his hips so that she could move against him. The taste of him on her tongue like honey, so sweet she couldn't get enough. She wanted to devour him.

He pulled away slowly and to her own embarrassment she let out a little growl, her body rising up to follow him, protesting against the loss of heat.

'There you are.' His smile was pure sin, his eyes dark mirrors of the wild desire she felt thrumming within her own chest. When he began undoing the zip of her dress, she helped him, their fingers a messy tangle of urgency. She laughed out loud when he gave up on decency and pulled it open the rest of the way with his teeth. He laughed too.

She marvelled at the fact that she was able to find humour in such an intimate moment and wondered if that was usual for a one-night deal. Maybe it was. She had always imagined a one-night stand to be something fast and thoughtless but this…this felt so right. The urge to ponder that pulled at her but she pushed it away, focusing her attention down to the fine point of contact between her abdomen and his hands. She watched him, watched his dark head lower as he peeled open the edges of her dress slowly, his big hands spreading over every inch of bare skin. She writhed, pleasure drugging her as his lips continued their slow descent along each part of her body he exposed.

'This dress has tortured me all evening. I can't count the times I have imagined doing this, unwrapping you like a mouth-watering delicacy.'

'You make me sound like candy,' she murmured, her breath catching as he paused just above the centre of her, shoving the skirt of her dress up above where her body pulsated and begged the most.

His eyes met hers for a split second, his pupils dark with desire as he drew her silk panties down her legs and his lips touched her core with the barest featherlight kiss. Then another. When his tongue joined in, she thought she might actually pass out from the pleasure. But he kept his hands firmly on hers, pressing down into her hips as he continued to devour her with relentless precision.

She felt the pressure building within her like an earthquake, small ripples followed by larger ones until she could feel her spine draw tight as a bowstring. It was too much and yet not quite enough, and the anticipation was such a beautiful torture she feared she might actually faint.

Xander paused, looking up at her like a dark angel with his lips parted and glistening.

'Show me what you need, Pandora.'

To her own shock she felt herself reach down one trembling hand to touch his jaw, moving him just the tiniest fraction to one side where the pleasure was deeper and more intense.

'Yes.' He murmured approvingly against her. 'Show me, *agape mou*. Let me get you there.'

She felt her release build again, this time with an intensity that had her body rising like a wave. He held her tight, keeping her steady as she finally cried out and shook with each blissful tremor and aftershock. When she finally stilled, he lifted his head, a look of victory on his face that shouted primal male satisfaction.

'The condoms are in my bag,' he purred, nibbling at her earlobe, sending shivers of excitement down her spine.

'Oh…' she murmured. *'Oh…'* Realisation dawning, she blushed. She'd almost forgotten again. The shoulders of her dress had already been pulled down, leaving her breasts exposed. With one quick pull, it finally landed in a pool of silk on the floor next to the bed.

She lay there completely naked, and his gaze drank her in. His face showed appreciation as only a man could. It made her blush but she made no attempt to hide herself. What was the point when he'd already had his mouth all over her?

Xander could hardly contain his need. Gone was the shy, reserved Pandora he once knew, leaving in her place this vixen who seemed determined to drive him utterly wild.

Her eyes were a mirror of his own, blazing with fire and need.

'Now.' Her whisper was urgent, said between shallow gasps for breath.

He needed no further encouragement. Pressing her down onto the bed with his body, he quickly removed the rest of his clothing before reaching down into his bag on the floor for protection.

He moved himself inside her in one slow thrust. They both moaned with relief from the final joining of their two bodies. He stayed still for a moment, afraid to break the sensation of pure pleasure coursing through him.

Her hips moved against him, her thighs spreading further apart, and he sank into her more deeply, beginning a rhythm of pleasure that was driving him higher and higher. Her body was all around him, suffocating him with need. Moving his head down, he sucked one hard nipple into his mouth. She gasped, a mixture of pleasure and pain, pulling him deeper inside her, wanting more.

His breath was laboured now, he couldn't hold on much longer. He could feel his stomach clenching. His balls tightening, ready to explode.

'Come for me…' she whispered throatily.

That was all it took, suddenly he was over the edge, exploding in a pleasure so delicious he could feel it in the tips of his toes. His body convulsed with the efforts of his orgasm and she ground her hips underneath him, drawing out his pleasure as she reached her own. He fell down beside her, drawing her into his arms, out of breath and elated from his release.

Pandora sat in the Kyoto house looking out of the window the following morning. Silence enveloped her and she instinctively wrapped her arms around her knees. They were flying back home from Osaka later today, once Xander returned from wherever he'd gone while she was still asleep. She looked at her watch. They were going to miss their flight slot if he didn't come back soon.

The morning outside was grey, a light drizzle making the mountains look as if they were gradually disappearing into the clouds. She wasn't sure how long she stayed in that position, staring out into nothing.

What would things look like once they were back in New York? Would he even speak to her unless it was for an event? The thought of their wedding looming, the ever-growing guest list she'd seen him scrolling through… Her stomach lurched. She felt shaky and off balance and she knew exactly who was to blame. Xander Mytikas had done nothing but unsettle her delicate equilibrium from the moment they'd met and she didn't just mean in the physical sense.

She'd never had a one-night stand in her entire life, the very idea of it went against everything she'd always thought she'd require in order to enjoy sex. But with Xander, it hadn't felt like a one-night stand at all. It had felt like finally walking through the right door after months of wandering around completely lost in the wilderness. It had felt like coming home.

She shook off that dangerous thought, knowing nothing good could come of it. In the end, she had simply taken what he'd been willing to give and they both knew it was the smartest choice. But a tiny part of her wished she had resisted, wished she didn't know what it felt like to have his lips on hers and his body stretching her own to its limits. She wished she were still wondering, unknowing, because she now knew that knowledge wasn't always power. She had never felt so utterly powerless in her life. She glanced at her watch again. It looked as if she might be flying back solo. She'd better get ready to leave.

But when she walked down the steps of the house with her suitcase, it was to see Xander's powerful form striding towards her.

'I had a few loose ends to tidy up with Ran Tanaka.' Xander frowned down at her suitcase. 'Where are you going? I was hoping you'd still be sleeping.'

'You weren't there when I woke up,' Pandora heard herself say, her voice flat as she continued to stare past his left shoulder. 'I thought perhaps you had decided on a clean break. No hard feelings. So I decided to head back to Osaka to catch the flight.'

'You thought I'd spent the night making love to you more times than either of us can remember and then just leave you to return to New York by yourself?' His eyes turned grave and serious as he reached for her hand.

Pandora took a step back, knowing if he touched her…especially if he touched her with the same kindness she could see in his eyes… she would be lost. She wanted to walk away from this impulsive, reckless mistake with her dignity intact, a feat that would be entirely impossible to achieve if she gave in to the wild impulse she had to simply throw herself into his arms.

But it seemed she didn't need to do that, because before she'd had a moment to react he had closed the space between them. His chest was almost flush against hers, his eyes bearing down upon her in a way that strangely reminded her of his angry office death glare. Was he planning to fire her as his wife already? Had he decided that winning his inheritance wasn't enough of a reason to endure her presence for the next twelve months?

'I never planned for us to sleep together in the first place and we both know it's probably a terrible idea to keep tempting fate, but clearly we are both completely unable to exhibit any self-control,' he said.

'Speak for yourself. I could totally stop any time I wanted to,' she retorted, lying for all she was worth.

His gaze turned gentle. 'I thought we might stay in Japan a little longer.'

Stay. The word was like a war cry within her, lighting up all the darkness that had begun to encroach. It seemed too good to be true, him asking her to stay and it meaning exactly what she wanted it to mean. 'For how long?'

'I don't actually need to be back in New York until next week for a board meeting. They can do without me until then. I haven't taken a vacation from the company in three years.'

'That's it, you just want a break?'

'I think we both deserve it, don't you? Consider it a celebration of our expansion. We can pass it off as wanting to extend our honeymoon. We are supposed to be madly in love, after all.'

Pass it off. Of course, they were still playing a part, weren't they? He was still thinking of how this would look to his board. How he could use it, spin it to his best advantage. His simple words hit her hard, making her almost accidentally reveal all her messy feelings in one terrible tide of truth. He wanted her, at least for now. And, God…she wanted him too. But still she held back, needing to protect herself.

'It has to be just for this week. Promise me, Xander.' Her body practically hummed like a tuning fork, struck boneless with desire for this impossible magnetic force of a man. But she needed to know exactly where the boundary was here, or her mind would ruminate endlessly over the possibilities. She'd lose herself in this, in him, unless she had a clear idea of what they were doing.

'I promise. I'm not looking for anything more,' he murmured softly against her earlobe, biting down to seal their deal.

He was her drug, there was absolutely no doubt about that. And she knew with absolute certainty that she would take whatever she could get of him while she could, and to hell with the consequences. She would deal with them later.

CHAPTER ELEVEN

THE ADVENTURE THAT Xander had planned turned out to begin with a full day exploring the wonders of Kyoto, followed by their arrival at a private train, which was to be their home for the next five nights. The car was the height of luxury, usually only available to eight individual guest parties with a minimum of a two-year waiting list for the privilege. Of course, Xander had managed to buy out the entire train for their own private use for the week with hardly any notice at all.

They had a private chef and a small staff, each of whom were an absolute delight in creating the most perfect authentic Japanese experience while they travelled along the famous Seto Inland Sea, taking in the most beautiful sights. Their bedroom had a wall of one-way glass that expanded almost across the ceiling and Xander had made quick time in getting them alone so that he could make love to her while the countryside passed by.

On their penultimate day, they stopped at Miyajima Itsukushima, a mountainous island covered in the most glorious shades of red and orange maple trees that were renowned across the country. It was a little like travelling back in time, Pandora mused as she watched a group of children walk ahead of them in school uniforms. No traffic lights guided the roads, only patience and courtesy. Even with the tourists there, it was still quiet enough to hear the breeze rustle the leaves and the birds chirping above. It was also home to a great many deer, which they found out when one almost trampled Pandora as she became too distracted looking up at the trees.

Xander simply tightened his hold on her, not admonishing her for her carelessness, which she appreciated. It still confused her how his caring touch and attentive gestures didn't feel like being minded. Of course, that was exactly what he was doing, minding her. But it didn't feel bad. It felt different, somehow.

Like how he had draped a blanket over her the night before when she'd fallen asleep while reading. Or when he had taken her by the hand and led her to the viewing deck for a romantic dessert date while the sun began to set. Or when he had made sure to leave her an extra vegetable gyoza at lunch today, because he instinctively knew that they were her favourite. Not to mention his selflessness and impeccable instincts in the bedroom…

Shaking off heated thoughts of the previous night, she focused on finding her footing on the uneven path and tried to recentre her sex-addled brain. But admitting the definite increase in the number of times that her husband had begun to feature in her thoughts and dreams didn't change the fact that Xander was still Xander.

He had made his position on their relationship quite clear right from the start, and she had been perfectly happy to take one week of mindless pleasure. She was fully prepared to return to New York afterwards and play the role she'd originally been assigned to.

They walked in silence along the path, wind rustling the trees all around them. Until finally they reached steep steps, rising above them like a mountain. By the time they reached the famous temple, a fine sheen of sweat had broken out all over her body but she felt strangely exhilarated. Knowing Xander was beside her had made her feel confident enough to simply push her own limits. Not once had she panicked or felt the urge to retreat.

But knowing that his strength had such an effect on her made that prickle of emotion in her heart burn all the more and she found she couldn't quite look at him without feeling the urge to throw herself into his arms.

Thankfully, Xander distracted her from such messy inappropriate impulses by launching into his knowledge of the shrine's history. In true Xander form, he had collated some research at some point before they'd left that morning, most likely while she'd been sleeping. They were such opposites in so many ways and yet when he eagerly explained the basics of the Shinto faith and the emperor who had chosen Miyajima as a sacred place, she couldn't help but be fascinated too.

His thirst for knowledge made him the perfect tour guide, but she liked to think that she took some of the edge off his controlling ways with her slightly silly questions and requests for off-path explorations. Where she was a little chaotic and distracted, Xander was observant and organised, and she had absolute faith that they would not get lost so long as he was in command. It was strange, trusting someone so blindly.

Even as a teenager travelling with her parents, she had always felt a level of anxiety that urged her to remain behind, to not relax too much. With Xander, she felt free. She felt as if she could let her mind wander and allow herself to truly embrace the scenery, knowing that he would be right there by her side to nudge her if she missed a step.

Now that she had experienced travelling with him by her side this way, she had no idea what life would be like without him. She imagined all her grand plans, travelling the world and being spontaneous… And it all just seemed so colourless.

Once their year was up, they would probably never see one another again. The thought hit her with such jarring force her footing wavered and she stumbled slightly. Xander caught her, of course. He had an uncanny talent for saving her from falling flat on her face. But suddenly, his touch on her elbow was too much. She found herself lagging behind as they explored, keeping a little more distance between them.

Just because they had decided to take this week to explore the sexual connection between them, didn't mean that he had suddenly changed his outlook on relationships, and she seriously needed to remind herself of that.

She was a grown woman, she reassured herself with a steely determination. She was not so weak that she would fall to pieces over a short fling with her temporary husband, right?

As they walked back down to the small sandy beach near the harbour, Pandora ignored the puzzled looks that Xander threw her way. She knew she was being too quiet. She could feel his curious gaze on her and see the puzzled look on his handsome face. But how could she even begin to explain why words were too much? Why she suddenly felt so sensitive and vulnerable?

She had got too comfortable, she realised. She had begun to sink into his strength like a balm, and that was something she simply could not afford to get used to. Fear of the unknown had always been a huge trigger for her, but, strangely, knowing exactly when this entanglement would end was far more of a torture.

She wasn't supposed to become attached. She had promised him that this short fling was exactly what she wanted. Maybe in the beginning, she had believed it herself too. But now, there was no denying the fact that it was going to destroy her when he gave her what she'd asked for. She hadn't even been in love with her first boyfriend when he'd broken up with her and she'd still struggled for a couple of weeks. Forming successful intimate relationships was a complex and intense process for her and so, naturally, the ending of such attachments was equally hard.

But she had survived being dumped by that weasel Cormac Nally, hadn't she? She'd picked up her pieces and moved to New York City, for goodness' sake, even if it had taken being blackmailed by Zeus to get her there. Maybe once this year was up and their divorce was finalised, she could move back to Japan for a while. She had become a rather seasoned traveller... almost. Okay, so she might still need a chaperone to avoid being trampled by the occasional sacred deer.

But she'd be fine.

She paused at a low wall, staring out at the calm sea as the evening began to darken. The light breeze soothed her skin and cooled her heated cheeks as she tried to calm herself. Her heart was beating a little too fast, her breath hurting a little as she exhaled on one long gust of breath.

Almost as though he sensed the emotional distance she was busy building between them, Xander moved closer. Strong arms enveloped her with warmth as the wind blew her hair around her face.

A confusing cocktail of emotions began to swirl in her chest, taking her completely by surprise. The term *heartache* had always seemed so ridiculous to her, and yet if it had been possible to feel actual pain in that vital organ she'd bet that this was what it would have felt like. Her chest squeezed with pressure, her throat dry and aching as she hid her face in the front of his sweater.

She breathed in, inhaling the scent of his cologne and skin as though she could use it to cement this memory in her mind for ever. Because she knew with sudden clarity that eventually memories would be all that she had left of their time together.

'You've gone quiet on me,' he murmured, his lips pressed against the side of her temple.

When she didn't immediately respond, he moved back a couple of inches, gently tipping her chin up to search her face. 'Hi.'

'Hello,' she responded, forcing an easy smile to her lips.

'Everything okay?'

'I'm feeling a little…off balance,' she said, shocking herself with the truth of her words. Surprised that she hadn't felt the need to lie to placate his feelings. Even more evidence that this relationship was more than anything she had ever thought a connection with another person could be. But, she supposed, she hadn't actually voiced that development to Xander. So she inhaled a deep breath and braced for the inevitable set-down.

'The past few days, it's been like living in a romantic comedy movie montage. The food and the laughter. It's been amazing, but I know that once we go back to New York… Once this truce is over, we go back to reality and I'm worried we'll go back to being…what we were.'

'You mean, you wonder if I'll go back to the

way I was?' he asked perceptively, his hands still on her, not breaking contact. 'The cold, aloof, removed bastard of a boss.'

'I've never seen you as cold.'

'I was a bit of a bastard, though?' He raised one brow.

Pandora felt a rush of laughter bubble up into her throat, despite the seriousness of the feelings swirling within her.

'Perhaps just a bit.' She smiled, biting down on her lower lip as he leaned forward and nipped her jaw playfully with his teeth. She turned her face away, feeling a little whiplash from his swift change from intimacy to humour.

For a long time, no words were spoken and yet his hands remained on hers as the sunlight began to wane and the ferry moved smoothly across the water. She felt the tiredness creep into her bones as they journeyed in silence through the twilight back to the railway station.

The staff greeted them with warm smiles and hot tea upon arrival. Their private carriage had been freshly cleaned and candles had been lit in preparation for another beautiful starlight supper. A light array of snacks had also been laid out on the dining table, including fresh fruits and sweet cakes. But Pandora had no appetite at all. Suddenly she felt the weight of her decision to enter into this brief affair with Xander descending upon her, with all the impossible consequences that she hadn't foreseen. She had thought she could be spontaneous and carefree, although she should have known better.

When Xander excused himself to take a call, she jumped at the chance to escape to the bathroom, splashing some cool water on her wrists and face. She didn't know how long she stood there, staring at her own reflection and trying to calm her erratic heartbeat but when she exited into the bedroom, Xander sat on the end of the bed, waiting for her.

'I just needed to get changed,' she said quickly, brushing her hair behind her ears and hoping that he didn't see the evidence of the tears she'd shed. But one look into his eyes and she knew that he'd seen.

'There's more to it than that,' Xander murmured. *'Agape mou*…talk to me.'

She closed her eyes at the endearment, knowing just enough Greek now to know what it meant. But she was not his love. She would never be his love.

She felt the final wall crumble within her and she met his gaze, her voice a breathy shiver.

'Maybe I'm just inexperienced, but I have no idea how people can share a bed for a week and then go back to normal. This kind of wild sexual abandon isn't normal for me.'

'This isn't normal for me either.' He paused, an uncharacteristic hesitation and hitch in his breath, and when he looked up at her she caught a glimpse of vulnerability in his expression that shocked her to her core. 'I knew that there was chemistry between us, but it's becoming quite the addiction.'

He stood quickly, reaching her in quick strides, and she felt his large hands cupping her cheeks. The single, solemn *'Quinn'* that he murmured against her temple was almost more than she could bear.

'Could you stop being so wonderful?' She swallowed past the lump in her throat and placed a playful punch on his biceps. 'Otherwise, when we get back to New York, I don't know how I'm going to be in a room with you and not want to climb you like a tree.'

A dark look entered his eyes for a split second, then it was gone and he was stepping closer and pulling her against him. He growled her name against the tender skin of her neck, lifting her tighter against him. Their bodies melted into one another like twin flames, and for a moment Pandora felt a little frightened by the intensity of it. The intensity of the passion that seemed to consume her every time he was near. It somehow managed to feel like too much and not enough, never enough.

She would never be free of him.

She closed her eyes and felt a single tear escape her lid, trailing down to fall into his silky salt and pepper hair. He didn't notice, he was too far gone as he licked and laved a trail down between her breasts. He lowered to his knees on the floor before her, his large hands a dark contrast against her pale hips as he pressed her back against the door of the cabin.

'Let me help?' He quirked one dark brow, his expression one of pure sin as he leaned in to press a single kiss against her lower abdomen.

Pandora shivered, her body melting into his caress. His hands were firm as he held her in place, taking one of her knees and hooking it carefully over his shoulder. The train was moving fast now, the world spinning past them in a blur. She closed her eyes as his mouth found its target and began to work, spiralling scorching hot pleasure along her limbs.

Even with her thoughts racing, her release came with shocking speed; the only thing stopping her from falling to the ground was Xander's strong arms holding her up. When she risked a glance downwards, he was watching her, his expression one she had never seen before. She felt the urge to cover herself or move away from that look, from the vulnerable and shaky feeling it evoked within her.

Time and time again this man had intimated that he was incapable of caring for others or falling in love, just like his father. But the way he cared for her, the way he made love to her... The way he was looking at her right now as he lifted her into his arms and carried her across the room to place her carefully on the bed... He murmured something unintelligible in Greek, pressing his face to her hair and inhaling deeply. The action seemed shockingly intimate, even in light of the many other, more scandalous things they had done together in the past week. She suddenly wished she had put more effort into learning his native language.

Of course, her first experience of falling in love would be with a man determined to keep her at arm's length. She closed her eyes in despair. She'd tried to protect herself, but it was far too late for that now. What had happened in Japan was going to have to stay in Japan. It was what she'd insisted on, after all.

'What's wrong?' Xander asked as he drew back and looked at her face.

'I've broken your rule,' she said simply.

Xander stilled, almost afraid to take another breath until she clarified that point.

'Broken my rule, how?' he heard himself

say, his body still and unmoving on the large bed. Pandora stood up, folding her arms over her chest and walking over to the window. The world whizzed by in a blur of red leaves and blue skies but Xander's gaze was glued to Pandora's face and the whirlwind of emotions passing through it one by one until she finally closed her eyes.

Not liking being blocked out, he stood up before he could even remind himself of all the reasons why he didn't really want to push her for an answer. Why he should leave her to compose herself and they could brush over her misstep and pretend it hadn't happened.

'I'm not just addicted to this, Xander. I'm…' She shook her head, swallowing hard before she turned back to face him. 'I'm in love with you.'

'No, you're *not*,' he responded, the reflexive answer escaping his lips before he had a chance to catch himself. He'd seen her wince at his words, seen the pain on her face even as she closed her eyes against it.

'Is it really so impossible to believe?' she asked. She shook her head, her eyes meeting his for the briefest seconds, before sliding away. 'I've…never said that to anyone before.'

His thoughts were consumed by the need to pull her back to him, to demand that they moved past this conversation and all the jagged edges it unleashed within him. Moments ago, they had been wrapped in one another—how had it come to this?

'I don't understand you,' she said. 'You have let Zeus take so much from you. He is dead, Xander, and yet you still use your fear of being like him to keep everyone at arm's length. I believe that your actions with Eros were not done out of selfishness, but of love. You don't have to keep shutting everyone out, Xander.'

He shook his head, words failing him as he reached for her. He would just kiss her, he decided. He would kiss away these doubts and remind her of what was good between them, what could still be good...

'No.' She pushed his hand away. Steel laced that single word, her shoulders squaring, shutting him out further.

Xander froze, his arm slowly dropping back to his side.

'I can't keep doing this. I will play my part when we return to New York,' she continued as he remained silent. 'But what has happened here in Japan between us...will stay here.'

'Is that what you want?' he finally gritted out. 'That we leave it like this?'

'I'm still technically your wife for the next

year. Did you expect me to just keep sleeping with you indefinitely?' She swallowed, her lower lip trembling. 'This is how it needs to end. I'm ending it.'

He looked up at the ceiling, rage threatening to consume him. He wasn't capable of returning her feelings, whatever she said. He'd never been cut out for relationships, he was too selfish, too cold and focused on growing his empire. He had seen what loving his father had done to his own mother, to most of the women Zeus had ever been with. To take Pandora's love would be to doom her to a life of heartbreak. She deserved somebody more worthy of her love than him, maybe someone closer to her own age.

Of course, she was right that this should end now, but he wasn't ready to do without the pleasure they'd found in each other's arms just yet. If that made him totally selfish, then so be it. He'd had nearly a week of making love to her, of waking up to her face each morning. This… infatuation should have begun to feel less intense by now.

He'd never had much willpower when it came to the things he enjoyed most and Pandora Quinn had become the most delectable dessert to his starved, sugar-crazed palate. But truthfully, he knew that if the choice was his…he wouldn't end it until they were both in ruins and she hated him for not being enough for her, for being unable to love her back the way she deserved.

So in the end, he simply nodded once, his own pride forcing him to walk away, even as hurt crossed her beautiful face.

CHAPTER TWELVE

PANDORA WINCED, STRUGGLING for the third time to comprehend what the handsome make-up artist was saying to her. The younger man frowned, looking over at his assistant with a thinly veiled exasperation. But just when she thought she was about to receive another snarky comment, the younger man directed his gaze at the woman who was blow-drying her hair to within an inch of its life. He made a small gesture towards the hairstylist and all at once the incessant noise in the room seemed to dip and Pandora let out a heaving sigh of relief.

Her thoughts had been a swirling vortex of anxiety all day. All contact with her husband over the past week since their return to New York had been limited to a few wedding-related email updates. He'd left every morning before she woke and not returned home until well after midnight. She should be glad that dealing with his brothers and the inheritance was taking up his time and giving them space in the aftermath of her mortifying declaration of unrequited love. She should be busying herself with her own plans to accept Ran's job offer once the wedding was over. But she couldn't stop herself from growing steadily more annoyed with Xander's ice-man demeanour, wanting to poke at him like a child at an anthill. If she'd thought he'd been difficult before, when he had simply been her boss...that was nothing compared to the intense way she caught him staring at her every time they had the misfortune of being together in the same room.

On one such occasion, she'd got into the elevator to attend her final dress fitting only to have him step in at the last moment. The tension on the long ride down to the ground floor from his penthouse had been almost unbearable. He'd asked her how she was doing with the wedding preparations and she'd responded honestly that she was feeling quite overwhelmed. He'd nodded, but said nothing more.

He had looked tired, and she'd longed to reach out and brush the hair from his brow. But she'd remained still and calm, both of them silent for the rest of the journey out to their separate chauffeur-driven cars.

The next day, she'd been assigned a virtual assistant to filter out the remaining calls and tasks that she could read through and confirm or amend via email. Other than today's final hair and make-up trial, she had nothing left to do other than show up on the day. There were no social events or dinners, no reason for her to stand by Xander's side and play the part of his adoring wife. She should be relieved he'd taken the pressure off, she realised. In a way, it felt strangely close to being cared for, though she knew that wasn't his intention. He was likely just trying to ensure there were no more embarrassing moments or public arguments to put the illusion of his perfect marriage in jeopardy.

Her thoughts were so busy, she almost didn't hear the huddled conversation going on between the make-up artist and hairstylist in the background.

'We can't both work on her at the same time, it will be too much for her,' the woman said, then winced. 'Poor girl is probably already uncomfortable.'

Pandora stiffened, no stranger to that particular tone of pity in the woman's voice and the answering dismissal in the other. They were discussing her as if she weren't here...as if she were a subject to pity and handle. That was it, she was being handled.

After experiencing the easy acceptance of her autism from people like Xander and Ran, the contrast was so glaringly obvious it made her grit her teeth, fuelling her determination as she turned in her swivel chair to pin the two beautiful people with her iciest glare. She smiled, of course, the kind of polite smile she'd seen Xander use in the past. He'd been the one to teach her that the strongest weapon she held was her integrity, after all.

And so she set them straight, grateful when they apologised and actually listened when she explained why it was inappropriate to assume things about her abilities or sensitivities.

'I'm so sorry.' The blonde looked embarrassed. 'My little nephew is autistic too, so I just presumed...'

'It's fine.'

It wasn't, really, but the woman looked so uncomfortable that Pandora just wanted to end the awkward moment. She almost didn't notice the most troubling part of the entire interaction was that the stylist had been acting this way from the moment she'd arrived, long before she might have noticed anything that might have tipped her off. She'd already known Pandora was autistic. How?

Frowning, she turned back and asked the question aloud, seeing the other woman's face tighten with discomfort.

'Oh. It was mentioned in the article that was posted the other day.'

'What article?' Pandora felt something sink

and tighten within her, like that moment when a plane lost turbulence and you dropped a couple of metres mid-air.

The two stylists looked at each other, and one of them picked up her slim tablet, tapping the screen a few times with her sharp red-tipped nails. Click, click, click. Pandora felt her teeth grinding against one another in the back of her jaw as she waited, her body filling with tension with each passing moment.

The tablet was placed on her lap and she looked down at a perfectly polished image of her own face smiling eagerly up into Xander's. She remembered that day at the gala, remembered her own nerves at being so close to him for the first time. She remembered how short and clipped he had been and wondered if he'd felt it too, even then. Of course, he'd admitted as much, hadn't he? He'd said he'd struggled to control his own reaction to her ever since that first night. But, of course, he'd also admitted that to her while they'd been in Japan. And all confidences of that nature had to be left behind there, as per their agreement...

Shaking her head, she refocused, scrolling down past the cover photo to the large headline that simply said *Heir of Zeus*. The article wasn't from a respectable business publication, but another magazine entirely and began with a heavy focus on Xander's handling of Mytikas Holdings in the face of his father's illness and passing. They mentioned Zeus as a powerful man but spoke nothing of his shady dealings, instead painting Xander as a rags-to-riches opportunist who had landed on his feet thanks purely to his gold-digging mother.

She lifted her hand to the lump of emotion that had formed in her throat, knowing the truth behind Xander's parentage and how it had affected him. She hated this article, hated whoever had written such thinly veiled words of jealousy and hate.

But then her eyes caught on her own name in the next paragraph and as she scrolled down another picture emerged. A picture of herself sitting at the formal dance held during her final year in university.

She told herself not to read any more, but still her finger pushed the text up, revealing a final paragraph containing details that were apparently sourced from 'someone close to the bride'.

...daughter of Irish senator Rosaline Quinn...gifted with languages...troubled teenage years...quirky and scatterbrained... autism spectrum disorder...

The final line of the paragraph questioned if Miss Quinn was built for the life of a society bride, and if Xander Mytikas was taking advantage of his meek, delicate secretary just as his own father had allegedly done numerous times with his own subordinates. Pandora closed the tab, feeling nausea swirl in her stomach and a slight rushing sound in her ears.

She was still sitting in the living room an hour later, in the exact same spot, when Xander returned from work. The penthouse apartment was silent and dark, and it took him a moment before he saw her. When he did, he rushed over, kneeling down on the carpet beside her where she'd been staring at her own picture in the terrible article.

'I was hoping you hadn't seen it yet.' He sighed, then seemed to debate for a moment before wrapping his arms around her. It was the first time they'd touched in several days, ever since they'd returned from Japan, and yet it felt like weeks.

As she relaxed against him, feeling the familiar heat of his lips tracing a path from her neck to her shoulder, she felt a surge of emotion catch her by surprise, tightening her throat.

When exactly had she begun to feel as if the world wasn't quite right if he wasn't nearby? It was a dangerous way to think, considering he would most definitely not be a permanent fixture in her life.

Her thoughts closed in on the sensual moment like a dark cloud on a rainy day, tightening a coil of anxiety within her that Xander proceeded to kiss away with his usual deftness. His eyes locked on hers for a split second and her breath caught with the intensity of feeling just looking at him stirred within her. She wanted to reach up and pull his face down to hers and kiss him until neither of them could breathe.

She wanted to kiss and lick every inch of his glorious body and memorise every line like her own personal map. As if she were a magnet and he had somehow become her true north. Fighting off the surge of anxiety over her whirling thoughts, she turned in the circle of his arms and sought his mouth, revelling in the deep groan that rumbled in his chest as their lips finally made contact.

Her kiss was not gentle. She felt his surprise as he gripped her waist, attempting to hold her to him and guide her rhythm but she refused. She needed to be the one in control right now. If they had nothing else, they at least had this wild sensual connection and she wanted a taste of being the one in the driver's seat of that runaway train for once.

As they flung off their clothes, she told herself she wanted to use him, to just take what she wanted like all the other modern, independent women. But even as she slid down upon his hard length and felt her body open to accept him, she knew she was only fooling herself. She still wanted so much more. The realisation only served to spur her on further, as if she might drive away the pain of her thoughts by riding him faster.

Xander reached up, holding her face in his hands, tethering her to him as he took control. His pace turned slower and deeper and as he thrust upwards he told her in a hoarse voice how beautiful she was. How wild she made him feel. How he could make love to her for hours. Words and phrases that made her foolish heart throb with longing.

She pushed the emotions down and focused on driving them both towards the peak. Xander's guttural moan of his impending climax was like a flip switch, shutting off all coherent thought. Her own orgasm was a full body quake that seemed to shatter her from the inside out. If she'd thought the lump in her throat had been hard to fight back, the sensation in her chest at that moment was almost more than she could bear.

Pandora awoke a while later to find Xander sitting up on the side of the bed, where they'd moved for a second round of passionate sex, his head in his hands, the picture of a man tortured. The sight of him made her sit up, covering herself reflexively.

'I wasn't going to apologise,' he growled. 'But I'm not a complete bastard, despite my previous actions. I've treated you badly, and you deserve better.'

'Yes, I do,' she agreed, satisfied when his eyes dropped to the ground. Let him feel some tiny bit of the pain he was causing her, causing both of them, by being completely closed off to what was so obvious to her. He might believe himself incapable of love and he might have very good reasons for believing that, but it was only fear holding him back. And if he wanted to badly enough, he could overcome that.

'I can't be what you need, Quinn.'

The use of her old nickname jarred her, poking a little hole in her fragile heart. Quinn again. She opened her mouth to reply, but the sky above them chose that exact moment to let out a rumble of thunder followed by a sharp flash that lit up his face.

Apparently he remembered how much she hated storms like this because he instantly reached out and took hold of her elbow, anchoring her. The gesture was so small and yet it touched her fragile heart, reminding her of all the other micro acts of care he seemed to perform reflexively. Damn, even when she was determined to hate this man he made it utterly impossible.

'You were apologising,' she breathed, cradling her own arms around herself and moving backwards on the bed to avoid her own impulse to lean into his touch. Or worse, to hug him. She wasn't sure how that would feel more intimate than the things they'd shared with one another already, but hugs had always seemed like the height of intimacy to her. Hugs were for family, close friends or lovers, none of which qualified as anything close to whatever she and Xander were to one another now.

'You made it clear that we were done when we left Japan. But when I walked in and saw you hurting like that…' He ran a hand over his unshaven jawline. 'I should have had more control.'

'I was a willing participant, Xander. Don't worry about it.'

Before she could fully break down, she strode into the en suite bathroom, locking the door behind her. She took more time than usual in the shower, refusing to cry as she washed her hair. When she eventually emerged into the bedroom, fully dressed once more, he was gone.

Not quite a professional relationship but a far cry from a true marriage—they seemed to have become stuck somewhere in between. She'd always hated grey areas, but that seemed the only logical way to categorise it. They were frozen, halfway between darkness and light. But no matter what way she looked at it, everything had changed between them most irrevocably.

Suddenly the idea of staying in this apartment for the next week, just waiting for her grand wedding, was like a slowly tightening noose. She should have accepted the job offer from Ran. If she had, maybe now she'd feel a bit more purpose and a bit less alone. The loneliness of being Xander's wife was suddenly more than she could bear. They were only a few weeks into their marriage—could she really survive an entire year feeling this way?

Allowing her impulse free rein, she clicked open her phone and started a video call, feeling butterflies swoop and flutter in her stomach. She closed her eyes, twirling the bracelets on her left wrist as the call connected and Ran's perfectly made-up face appeared on screen.

'I want to take the job,' Pandora said quickly, knowing she needed to get the words out and stay in control of the storm about to break inside her. 'If it's still on offer.'

'Of course it's still on offer. I always get what I want.' Ran smiled, triumphant.

Pandora tried to smile, but felt it go wrong. Her face seemed to crumble, her lips wobbling and her eyes filling with embarrassing tears. It was humiliating that Ran wanted her more than Xander did right now.

Ran frowned, peering closer at the screen. 'What happened?'

'I'm fine.' She shook her head and gasped, feeling her chest shudder. 'I'll be fine… I just needed to call you. You said if I changed my mind, I could take the job. I was thinking I could start working remotely. I just need…something.'

'I can do better than just something.' Ran sat up straight. 'The Tanaka jet's in New York. I'll have them wait for you and you can fly out first thing tomorrow.'

It was only once the arrangements had been made and she was left alone in the silence once again that she crumbled and felt herself break.

CHAPTER THIRTEEN

XANDER BARKED ONE final order at his chief operating officer and pressed the button for the privacy glass that surrounded his office. The replacement translator had made a couple of crucial mistakes on the final contracts for the Tanaka deal and it had created a twenty-four-hour panic to rectify before it was officially announced to the press yesterday.

After a morning of media interviews where he'd dodged question after question about his wife and her whereabouts, he was once again feeling the urge to hit the gym and punch things. A full week of arguments and subtle attempts at sabotage by the mutinous board over his actions in Japan had exhausted him, but, no matter how tired he was from eighteen-hour days, the minute he lay down, his thoughts always returned to Pandora.

He hadn't spoken to her since she had walked away from him that night in his penthouse. She'd sent him an email early the next morning informing him of her plans to leave for the job in Japan, but by the time he'd got out of the emergency board meeting, Ran Tanaka's jet had already been flying high above the clouds. Not that he would have stopped her, of course. Besides the fact that she had no personal commitments in New York, she had every right to want her space from him. He had been nothing but distant from her since Japan.

Her decision to end their liaison had been logical, of course, but tell that to the dark part of him who didn't give a damn if their agreement was jeopardised. Her confession of love had scorched him to his bones, making him tighten his hold on her as though he could reshape her feelings into something less dangerous through sheer force of will. But in not responding in kind, he'd hurt her even more deeply than he'd realised.

He leaned back in his chair, closing his eyes at the infuriating reminder that this distance between them was not only necessary but essential. He'd just had his own things moved to Zeus's town house, where he would stay for the remainder of their marriage. It was only eleven more months…after which point she would be free to go. Free to move on and find someone more in touch with their humanity. Someone who wasn't a workaholic with a grouchy temper and an inability to fall in love.

The image of his wife with another man suddenly had him standing up on his feet and contemplating heading up to the office gym to assault a punching bag. He inhaled deeply, pacing to the windows on stiff legs, and stared out at the dark clouds gathering above the city.

He had spent the past week rushing through his days at the office, unfocused and irritable with his new assistant as he'd counted down the days to today when she would return for their rehearsal dinner. Tonight, they would hold a small dinner and then tomorrow was the larger event. But now, knowing that she was only an hour away at their Hamptons venue waiting for him… he felt nothing but unease.

He'd seen glimpses of her exploring Tokyo through periodic checks of Ran Tanaka's very popular public social media feed. She looked happy and bright, far from appearing to be experiencing the same dark irritability he'd been subjecting his own staff to in her absence. Seeing her clear bond with her new friend, he was jealous. The guilt assailed him when he thought of his initial reaction to her job offer and how he had wanted to convince her to turn it down. He hadn't outright demanded that she return to New York to be by his side, but he'd wanted to. He'd wanted to convince her to stay with him, in his bed, wrapped around him.

And so he had stalked the corridors of his office like a coward, knowing that if he didn't keep himself busy, he'd do something stupid. Such as follow her to Japan and beg her to come home. He'd learnt long ago that it was always better to maintain control of such situations and avoid weakness. Pandora Quinn was most definitely a weakness to him, no matter how much something inside him railed against the thought.

He growled under his breath, twirling his wedding ring around on his finger. This break apart was exactly what they had both needed. Things had got too intense in Japan, too…domestic. He had become entirely too comfortable waking up alongside her every morning, working together, exploring together. Was it any wonder that things had gone as far as they had?

With his workaholic tendencies and impatient nature, he had long ago decided that he had no interest in a family of his own. A choice that had only cemented in his mind as he learned of the devastation his father had wrought on the women in his life. Pandora's words haunted him, her perceptive comment that he used his father's evil misdeeds to reinforce the wall he had built around himself and push people away. But she was wrong about his reasons for doing so; he wasn't protecting himself, he was protecting her. He was giving her a chance to truly find happiness with someone who truly deserved her love.

With distance would come clarity for them both…and sanity.

But today was the day she had returned, tonight would be their wedding rehearsal and tomorrow he would stand in front of a crowd of people he barely knew and cement his position as one of them. Their wedding guest list included politicians, actors, even a couple of well-known rock stars. It was the kind of PR power move that he had long dreamed of.

The elite events team he'd hired had planned the weddings of royalty but still Xander had ensured certain accommodations were made for his bride. The team had been discreet and thorough, even arranging for a full run-through of the ceremony before the event itself.

Pandora had assured him that she was prepared for the pressures of such a large event and despite his own reservations he knew she would be. So why then did he suddenly wish they had planned something smaller? Something more intimate? Something…real.

The thought jarred him, making him rock back on his feet for a split second. He knew the terms of their marriage. He had set them, after all. They both knew what this was and what it could not be. Why then did he have the sneaking feeling that he had decided, in his usual way, that she somehow had become his?

He knew that was ridiculous, Pandora was not an object to be possessed, but whenever he thought of their deadline divorce date looming in the not-too-distant future…

But before he could finish up his working day and head off to the Hamptons, he had to deal with one minor annoyance in the form of his brother's arrival in his office. He made Eros wait, his usual move when he wanted to maintain control of a meeting. Eros might be his brother but, as far as he was concerned, this was not a house call. There would only be one reason for Eros to come here when Xander had already had word that he'd been spotted in the Caribbean on honeymoon with his new wife.

As he stalked into the room to face Eros, he waited for any hint of resentment or anger at the fact that his brother had married his ex-fiancée, but nothing came. His and Priya's match had been short-lived and strictly professional, after all. To his own surprise, he bit back the urge to congratulate his brother on his nuptials, but then remembered that they were still technically rivals in this race.

'You look…tanned,' he said simply.

'You look like death warmed up. Clearly marriage has affected us in very different ways, brother.' Eros quirked one brow, leaning back in his chair in a way that made Xander's teeth grit hard.

Though there were only six years between them, Xander had always envied his younger brother's youthful energy. He remembered the first day they met, and Eros had introduced himself loudly as the other bastard, much to their father's horror. They hadn't always been rivals. In fact, he would go so far as to say they had been friends once. Until Xander had been forced to make a choice that still haunted him to this very day.

'I hear you've neglected to invite me to yet another one of your weddings?'

'If you came here to ask for an invite, you could have just emailed.'

'Don't worry, your wife already ensured we were sent an invite. Priya has been video-calling her about renting office space when she returns to the city.'

Xander stilled. His wife and the woman who'd jilted him were working together? But strangely, it felt…nice. He imagined a future where he and Eros ran in the same circles once more, perhaps even had a friendly dinner party with their wives. Would it be strange?

He shook off the thought, knowing it was far

too early to entertain such thoughts. He didn't even know why Eros was here. He crossed his arms, staring out at the view he had coveted for most of his adult life, the view that was now his so long as he maintained control of the board. Eros had already informed him he'd forfeited his right to the inheritance; Nysio was still unmarried and determined to remain unconnected to the Mytikas name.

'I have a wedding rehearsal to attend shortly,' Xander said stiffly.

'Well, then, allow me to get straight to the point.' Eros stood up. Placing his tablet on the conference table, he tapped the screen a few times, then extended it for Xander to take a look.

Xander peered down, taking a moment to make sense of the charts and projections in his brother's trademark chaotic organisation. But then he realised exactly what he was looking at…and his blood turned cold.

'Arcum…' he gritted. 'You mean to tell me that the shadow corporation that's been buying up Mytikas shares all over this city—that was you?'

'That is correct. And you are Titan Corp.' Eros's face was devoid of humour for once, his expression one of utmost seriousness that reminded Xander of…himself.

'How did you come by this information?'

'For the past ten years, I've made it my business to know everything that my enemies have done.'

Taking a deep breath, Xander scanned the charts again. 'If you are here to leverage me or try to buy me out...'

'Let me clarify. Things are not the same now as they were fifteen years ago. Zeus is dead and through my relationship with Priya I've come to realise a great many things. She made me realise, rather.' He smiled ruefully, then straightened. 'I'm not here as your enemy, Xander. I'm here as your brother. I've contacted the Italian too. I have a plan to propose that I think may just change everything for all of us.'

And so Xander found himself seated side by side with his brother for the first time in more than a decade as Eros outlined the details of his proposal to conspire with his brothers in a coup that would shock the business world for evermore. Together they controlled the majority shares of Mytikas Holdings.

It was scandalous, it was aggressive...it was brilliant.

Zeus had always made it clear that his youngest son would have been his first choice to carry on the Mytikas name. Though technically Xander had been given the powerful name at birth by his socially reaching mother, he hadn't truly felt as if it was his until Eros had left. With no one else there to challenge him, his victory had felt hollow.

His resentment for Zeus had only grown, fuelling him to investigate the accusations of corruption himself. Unlike Eros, Xander had the patience and foresight to play the long game. On the surface, he had been the dutiful son, Zeus's right-hand man. But beneath all his blind faith he had been laying the foundations for this very moment. He had trapped the beast that was Mytikas Holdings in a snare of its own corruption and, in doing so, he had aimed to make himself their only possible saviour. But taking the glory for himself had never been the plan. He hadn't been the only person that Zeus had hurt and therefore he wasn't the only one who deserved a chance at retribution. His brothers did too.

'What you are proposing is unheard of.' Xander finally spoke after a long silence.

'I don't expect you to trust me,' Eros said, his features hardening. 'But considering our history, I didn't need to bring this to you at all.'

There it was. Xander let out a slow breath at the reminder of his actions. The reminder of the bitter rivalry that had cut short their tentative bond of brotherhood years before.

'When I ran you out of New York, it was because Zeus had already found out what you'd uncovered. He planned to make an example of you. To teach you a lesson by implicating you in a corruption case that would have possibly cost you years of freedom. I chose your freedom over brotherhood. I knew that you would never forgive me or believe me if I tried to tell you the truth.'

'You're telling me that you weren't trying to get me out of the way?'

'Maybe it started that way—I am a selfish bastard in many ways. But I realise now that I made the wrong choice. I'm sorry, I should have told you and then let you fight your own battle.'

'Did you just…apologise to me?' Eros raised an incredulous brow. 'Marriage must have really done a number on you.'

It had, Xander realised. Pandora had been the one to sow the seeds of all this openness and communication and forgiveness. He knew now that if Eros hadn't come to him, he would have sought him out anyway to make this same apology. Because he meant every word.

He looked at the man he'd spent so long hating and memories of their short-lived brotherhood returned. He'd played it cool back then but his time working with his brother had been the happiest in his memory. They'd been a seamless working machine, both driven by the desire to improve things at their father's company. He wondered how their relationship might have grown and developed if he hadn't been so focused on proving himself to be more than just a consolation prize as a son.

Eros was silent, the only sound the dull tick of the grandfather clock in the hall. Then he stood and began striding towards him. Xander exhaled in shock as he was enveloped in a brief brotherly embrace.

'You know what this means, don't you?' Eros said.

'Yes, that with our combined shares we have control over Mytikas Holdings regardless of the rest of the board.'

'So you can let your wife go.'

'What?' Xander exclaimed in shock.

Eros looked taken aback. 'I'm sorry, I just assumed that your marriage to Pandora was the same arrangement as the one you had with Priya, one of convenience just to win the inheritance.'

'I have an arrangement with Pandora, yes.' He spoke the words, hating the sound of them as they came out of his mouth. Hating how wrong they felt. But it was the truth.

'Really? You don't sound convinced,' Eros mused. 'If that's the case, I'm sure she will be happy to be let off the hook and get her pay-off early.'

'Pandora is not just some gold-digger and I won't have her thought of that way,' Xander warned darkly, walking away and pinching the bridge of his nose. 'I wasn't prepared for any of this, but you're right about the combined shares—it makes perfect sense. I'd be a fool not to join forces with you. I just… I need a moment to think over all the angles.'

'Why do I get the feeling that you're not just thinking about the company right now?' Eros surveyed him with shrewd interest. 'Will this impact your fancy nuptials tomorrow?'

'She deserves to be released from our contract, yes. It's the best solution for everyone involved.'

'Ah.' Eros nodded once. 'Spoken like a man in love.'

Xander froze, his stomach tensing uncomfortably. 'Don't be ridiculous.'

'It sneaks up on the best of us.' Eros clapped him on the back. 'Do me a favour, go and talk to your wife before you take any action on this. Trust me, I learned my mistake the hard way on that one.'

Xander nodded, his mind moving quickly over all the details and changes, trying to navigate it all. He hardly noticed himself saying goodbye to his brother, who promised to see him at the wedding. He hardly noticed anything at all, other than the increasingly uncomfortable sense of dread filling his chest with every minute that passed.

The feeling persisted as he travelled to the helipad on the roof of Mytikas Holdings. Clearly, he was not as okay with this new development as he'd thought.

As had been made clear in countless meetings this week, this society wedding was a pivotal moment for Mytikas Holdings and his plans for the future as their CEO.

But now, in light of his conversation with Eros…all of that had changed. He could take over everything on his own terms. As far as moments went, this was huge, the culmination of a decade of strategising. But strangely, he felt no urge to celebrate.

Pandora had been in Japan for the best part of a week, not that he'd counted, of course. He simply kept track of such things. But even as he tried to convince himself of that truth, he felt the impatience and need to see her growing within him. He'd been like this all week, distracted and irritable, his thoughts consumed by soft porcelain skin and her stunning silver eyes. But it wasn't just her body he'd missed. It was everything about her. She'd unknowingly become the brightest part of his day from the moment they'd begun working together. He'd savoured their arguments and her set-downs and he'd valued her opinions and sharp mind.

What on earth had happened to his plans for a cold marriage of convenience?

Even trying to minimise what they had shared during that week in Japan was useless; his mind knew the reality. It was never just about sex or physical attraction with Pandora. What they had was so much more, it practically consumed him.

It was madness. It was dangerous. But he couldn't seem to make himself stop wanting her with him. Not just for one more night or one more week or even one more year…but as a permanent fixture. He couldn't imagine his life without her in it, but when had that happened? When had she become something so intrinsic to his happiness?

Eros's words seemed to float through his mind, taunting him. *Spoken like a man in love.* He stiffened at the thought, reflexively pushing it away. In his world, love had only ever meant weakness and vulnerability. It was the arrow you gave to another person to slice through your heart on a whim. It was weakness.

But the look on Pandora's face when she'd spoken those words to him on the train in Japan… she hadn't looked weak. She had been glorious. Her silver eyes incandescent and aglow with the terrible truth of her heart, even when he'd tried to extinguish that flame. His fists tightened on his knees as he leaned forward, his forehead pressing hard against the cold window of the helicopter as the city lights began to blur in the distance below.

This was madness, thinking that a man like

him had any right to her heart. He had broken her enough already and for once he would do the right thing. If she was no longer bound to him through their deal, she would be set free.

He needed to set her free.

Pandora rose from her chair, taking in her appearance with swift efficiency and calmly telling the stylist that she would finish dressing alone.

If they had any complaints, they didn't voice them. The kind-eyed make-up artist took charge in shooing them out and made sure to ask her if she needed anything before he left himself. Then she was alone, in blissful silence.

She felt a coldness settle over her as she focused on removing some of the heavier make-up and curling her hair around her face. Simple pink pearl earrings adorned her ears and a matching necklace sat just above her collarbone. The dress she'd chosen for the rehearsal was a blush pink shift that teamed beautifully with flat golden pumps that sparkled in the light as she turned from side to side before finally leaving the confines of her room.

Show time.

She was infinitely glad that she hadn't been pressured to wear heels as the steps already felt unsteady beneath her feet as she descended. Her heart thumped hard in her chest as she spied Xander waiting for her in the foyer of the venue, his back turned as he studied the glass in his hands. Whiskey, she realised with disappointment. Was he dreading the spectacle of pledging himself to her in front of his precious society? Was he worried she would embarrass him and his image?

For a moment, she briefly contemplated running back to her room to compose herself, but then he looked up and their eyes locked and she felt something within her melt.

She had seen Xander in a suit a thousand times since the day they'd first met, but the look on his face was what caught her breath. There was a level of heat there that seemed to burn through the fabric of her dress, touching her very heart. It should be a crime for a man to look the way he did in this moment.

She reached the bottom step and he was right there, taking her hand in his but not pulling her any closer. The foyer was just filled with a handful of staff members, readying the place for the rehearsal dinner. There was no need to put on a show. Yet she ached to reach up and touch his jaw, to kiss his lips and get carried away in that electric heat of desire that always seemed to end with them in a tangle of limbs in a bed, on a desk or even on the floor on occasion.

But something was different today. For someone who had always struggled to read people's meaning in their words, she had always been extra sensitive to their moods. But with Xander, it sometimes felt as if he had become an extension of her, as if she could feel his energy simply by being in the same room as him. In Japan, that feeling had only intensified, making her lose focus and fuelling her anxiety whenever he'd behaved in a way she hadn't expected. Like right now.

'You look beautiful,' he said, guiding her along the hall that led to the outdoor ceremony area. He paused just before they exited the double doors, where their celebrant waited along with the events team. Xander had made sure to send Pandora detailed reports of every decision that was made, ensuring that she knew what to expect. Slowly she had begun to understand the enormity of what she had agreed to. This was to be a finely executed event. But it would be okay, she told herself.

Xander would be by her side. She was simply playing a different role, just like the ones she had played all her life. The roles that smoothed out her edges and made her more palatable to others, the masks she wore to stop herself from standing out or being an embarrassment to the people she cared about. And she did care about Xander, probably far more than was sensible for a woman who had entered into a marriage with a one-year expiry date.

One year.

During her time alone in Japan she had stopped thinking about the fact that they had set a limit on their arrangement. But clearly he'd never forgotten.

She had never dreamed of more for herself than her studies and visiting her family, challenging herself to move to new countries and adapt. She had been content before meeting Xander, before he had shown her just what it meant to feel connected with someone in such a primal way. She felt as if before their first kiss, she had just been existing. From the moment his lips had touched hers, he had unleashed something inside her. He had opened up some hidden box within her soul and now there was no way to put it all back again. But still, a foolish hope stubbornly bloomed within her, growing and moving towards him like a flower seeking the sun.

It wasn't fair to him, putting him in such a position. He had never offered to be her sun or her moon. He hadn't even offered to be her husband, in truth. They had gone from a fraught working relationship to the tentative alliance of their temporary marriage then somehow had become lovers before either of them had had the chance to catch their breath.

They walked out into the evening light and she was stunned to see the ceremony had been completely set up in the few hours she'd been holed away upstairs with the styling team. The long lawn now boasted satin-covered chairs and flower stands spilling over with yellow roses. Her breath caught. Had he done that? The idea that he would request her favourite flower on purpose was a reach, the more likely situation was that an event planner had chosen them in pure coincidence. But the lawn was spilling with them, fragrant arrangements filling every corner.

Love for him filled her chest and she fought the urge to claim him once again, to demand that they give up on this foolish charade made up of restraint and rules that she knew neither of them wanted.

Xander might care about the propriety of their arrangement, but she didn't. Call her impulsive, but if this was a terrible decision, she wanted to dive in head first.

What if this connection between them was meant to be more, what if this marriage was meant to be real? The moment she felt the question take shape in her mind, she felt it fill up and expand. She couldn't marry him like this, she couldn't give up on the chance that they might actually be something to one another outside this deal.

She felt the pressure of reality weighing her down with every step, crushing her with expectation and responsibility.

Suddenly her feet refused to move.

She heard Xander ask if she was okay as though he were on the opposite side of a wall, while her thoughts swirled and caved in upon her with raucous vengeance.

The event planner smiled brightly, explaining that the usual series of vows would follow. The woman's shrill excited voice was impossible to keep up with, along with the banging from the chairs still being arranged on the lawn. So many chairs. So many strangers, watching her, wondering how on earth someone like her had wound up married to a handsome Greek billionaire.

Quirky and scatterbrained...autistic spectrum disorder...

'I'll get you to stand right here.' The woman nudged Pandora lightly on her shoulder, placing her at an angle to Xander's left. Pandora felt her mind grow foggy with the effort of withstanding her own panic. Still, the event planner continued to chatter mindlessly while Xander nodded, his hands stuffed into the pockets of his designer trousers. She focused on the watch upon his wrist, noting how dull the metal looked. How out of place it seemed. Was this how people would always see her? She had thought she was immune to the pain of being an object of public speculation. But that was before...

Before she'd realised that it wasn't just her that was affected by public opinion of their marriage. By the public opinion of her. Before she'd cared about Xander's happiness so much, a happiness that was directly affected by his social reputation.

The thought came with blinding clarity, like a sudden beam of torchlight. Painful and impossible to ignore. She knitted her hands together, wondering how on earth she had ever thought she could maintain the façade of a perfect wife for him. It would be laughable, really, if it weren't so impossibly sad.

'...and then I will ask you, Pandora, if you're ready to take this man as your husband, and you, of course, say—'

'No.'

She looked up from the anxious twist of her fingers and realised, by the number of eyes on them, that she had said it out loud.

She poised to apologise, to retract that tiny damning syllable. She didn't want to let him down. Didn't want to hurt him...or his reputation more than she already had.

But the words she knew she needed to say to smooth the moment over wouldn't come and, with every passing second of awkward silence, she felt the tension tighten, suffocating her.

CHAPTER FOURTEEN

XANDER TOOK ONE look at Pandora's face and knew he couldn't hold off on this conversation until after dinner, it needed to happen now.

She looked exhausted, he realised. A few loud bangs sounded out as a couple of waiters moved a table and he saw her wince. He fought the urge to growl at the men to leave, at everyone to leave. But he held back, politely asking the coordinator to empty out the marquee and give them some time to talk. It took a few torturous minutes to send away the team and waitstaff in the vicinity, a few minutes of watching Pandora shut down more and more with each second that passed.

Then suddenly, for what felt like the first time in weeks but was only a matter of days…they were alone.

Xander inhaled a deep breath, his mind wrangling the thoughts and feelings within him and pondering which combination of words might achieve the best result. Which magic phrase would allow him to let her go, to undo all the tangled wires of deceit and demands that had criss-crossed between them and at least have them parting on good terms.

But it was Pandora who spoke first.

'I'm sorry, Xander. I thought I was fine.' She half laughed sadly, a sound he found he didn't like at all. Her voice was barely more than a whisper. 'But then I saw my own face spread across a newspaper article.'

'I didn't approve any of the research performed on your family or you.'

'I know, you would never do that.' She met his eyes. 'It's not even about that… It's just being in Japan alone, without you… I had a lot of time to think. I had some things I wanted to ask you, but we had no time alone and now all this is happening. It's overwhelming.'

He'd seen it in her face, in the tense line of her shoulders. Even hearing her dismiss that cursed article as not being his fault made him angry. Of course it was his fault. Everything about her current situation had been caused by him or his family name, all of it.

He circled her wrist with his thumb and forefinger, the warmth of her skin sending a jolt of fire through him, but he let her go abruptly. He knew what he needed to do, knew that he couldn't keep her trapped in this life when it wasn't going to make her happy.

'I had a meeting with Eros today.'

Her eyes met his, surprise and a tiny hint of fear glimmering in their grey depths.

'There was no bloodshed. It was quite civil, actually. I…missed him.'

'Xander, that's wonderful,' she breathed, emotion glimmering.

'I realised how difficult I've been in the past, in refusing to change my opinions on certain things. Apparently, I can be quite stubborn.' He raised one brow and saw her expression soften with amusement. Still, he felt as if he stood on the edge of one of those circus ladders, high above the ground. He needed to do this, needed to tell her the full truth of her options. She'd said she loved him once and he'd pushed it away like a fool. What he'd give to hear it again from her right now. But he couldn't be selfish, he couldn't hold her tight like a spoilt child; she was not an object for him to possess. She was not his wife in truth; she had been forced into the position. Now it was time to give her the choice she deserved.

'Eros owns the company that we have been investigating for a while. Arcum. Apparently I wasn't the only one gathering shares using a shadow company. If we were to join forces, with the considerable percentage of shares we hold between us, we can stage a complete takeover of Mytikas Holdings. We could take everything.'

'And in doing so, you could bypass the terms of the will,' she said softly, her eyes not quite meeting his as she chewed at her bottom lip.

'I never had an interest in the rest of Zeus's estate anyway. Just the company.'

'Can you trust Eros?'

'Yes… I think I can. After all these years, it's become clear that Zeus deliberately kept us at each other's throats.'

Pandora was silent as she nodded, and he allowed her a moment to process the words before he proceeded.

'I suppose what I'm trying to say is that I know you don't want all this, Pandora. The big society wedding, the newspaper articles, the circus that is my life. I know that I have been asking a lot of you from the beginning…' He paused and ran a hand through his hair. 'These past few days, I realised some things and I…'

'You wanted to find a way out of all this,' she finished for him.

'Yes,' he said, then frowned. 'Not out of this entirely, just out of the part where I demanded that you be my wife for twelve months. Pandora… I think back to that night and I am so deeply ashamed at myself. At how heavy-handed I was, how I judged you and blamed you for everything. You deserved better from me and I can only hope you'll come to forgive me. That's why I'm setting you free from our deal. I will have divorce papers drawn up as soon as possible and you will still receive the financial settlement we agreed upon.'

Pandora made a tiny, strangled sound and when he looked down at her he could see she was shaking her head, the strangest expression on her face.

'Are you laughing? I'm making a very serious speech here and you're somehow amused by all this?'

'The exact opposite. I'm frankly amazed at the fact that I was just about to...' She shook her head, the tiniest hitch in her breath the only outward sign that she was not amused at all. 'You never contacted me, the entire time I was in Japan with Ran, apart from sending over information about the wedding. It's like you weren't even affected by anything that happened between us. And now you've decided on all this without even asking me what I want. So yes, I'm entitled to be upset.'

She was...upset? Hope bloomed in his chest like a weed, careening up the stony walls around his heart and finally crumbling them to dust. She had already told him that she loved him once...was he a fool to think that her love hadn't completely died when he'd behaved so badly? He'd acted out of fear before, he had practically pushed her to leave. But now…he felt the significance of the moment stretch out before him like a murky precipice. There was no guarantee that she wouldn't still walk away, but he had to try. He had to take that leap of faith and trust it wouldn't destroy him.

Quickly, he stepped in front of her, blocking her from walking away from the raised podium they stood upon. He looked around them at the rose-covered archway and the candles flickering in the light twilight breeze.

Pandora felt the last tiny ember of hope she'd clung to that he'd missed her while she was gone over the past week fade, giving way to a torrent of white-hot anger. How *dared* he? He had the gall to insist on this preposterous marriage deal in the first place, and now, barely a month later, when she was no longer useful to him, he was abandoning her as quickly as he could?

It had felt as though his words had come at her like arrows, hitting her squarely in the chest.

She shouldn't feel so hurt by his offer of a divorce. It had always been going to happen in less than a year's time. But hearing him say it so cavalierly, so soon, surrounded by this ridiculous wedding tent and what felt like a million of her favourite roses…she felt the last final piece of her heart shatter.

Unable to look up at him, she let the cold numbness that had threatened her all day finally take hold, steeling her features to blankness. Protecting her from falling down into a huddled pile of pain at his feet. But suddenly, the realisation of the ridiculousness of their situation dawned on her and she felt a semi-hysterical bubble of laughter escape her lips.

She covered her face with embarrassment, wishing she could simply click her fingers and return to the solitude of her room to have what was probably going to be a spectacular breakdown of sorts. She felt Xander move forward, the heat of him pressing along her bare arm making her jump with surprise.

'Pandora…please, don't cry. God, I'm messing all this up.' He touched her hands, concern lacing his voice for a split second. 'Wait, you're… laughing?'

'Sorry, I'm just…this is completely ridiculous.' She shook off his hand as another bubble of laughter escaped her chest, sending a tear down her cheek. 'We're starring in our very own soap opera here. You do know that, don't you? The jilted groom, jilting his replacement bride at the altar.'

He frowned at her words, looking almost hurt,

which made absolutely no sense considering he was the one ending things between them. She felt unhinged and exhausted and, God, why was he still looking at her that way?

'Jilting?' he echoed. 'Do you honestly think I would do that to you?'

She paused, something about his tone making her stand very still. He stood under the archway, looking like every fantasy bridegroom in her wildest dreams. But it was the look in his eyes that made her swallow hard. In all the months they'd worked together, she had never once seen Xander Mytikas admit fault or apologise the way he'd apologised to her tonight.

He'd practically begged for her forgiveness. And now, looking at him, steadfast under the arch where they'd been set to pledge their vows… She wondered if perhaps she'd got it all wrong. Still, she couldn't quite bring herself to ask him. That small, shaky part of her had already taken a catastrophic bruising. So she did the next best thing and uncrossed her arms, letting them lie flat at her sides. She took one step towards him, then another, until finally they were only slightly more than arm's width apart.

'I don't think you would hurt me like that on purpose, Xander,' she said softly. 'But the truth of the matter is, there is no reason for us to remain married now. I don't even work for you any more.'

'Without the deals and obligations…you can't think of one reason why we should?' he asked hoarsely.

He reached out and took her left hand in his, his thumb rubbing over the polished platinum rings on her third finger. 'You want to know why I've been quiet? Why I have barely been able to trust myself to be around you without an audience? It's because I've been wracking my brain to try to find a way to keep you. I just didn't think I deserved you.'

'Oh.' The single syllable left her on a rush of breath and she felt the world slow right down to a fine point. Everything else fell away and suddenly all she could see was Xander. For the first time since she'd walked down the steps, she looked at him, really looked at him.

There were fine lines of pressure around his mouth and a tiny unshaven patch of hair just under his ear, he had dark circles under his eyes and he looked thinner, as if he'd been exercising too much and forgetting to eat. Goodness…he looked just as terrible as she felt. How had she not noticed that?

All this time she'd been operating under the impression that she had been the fool who had fallen face first into love, but now as she looked into his eyes… That tiny spark of hope winked back to life within her chest once again.

'Knowing you were across the world in Japan this past week has been the most tortured I've felt in a long time. I know why you left. You are immensely talented and passionate and you shouldn't have been sitting around waiting to be wheeled out as my society bride. I was selfish to not continue to use your tremendous talents. I'm so sorry. Your replacement is utterly useless, if that's any consolation.'

She opened her mouth to respond but felt his index finger press gently against her lips, his left hand reaching for hers, his thumb smoothing over the rings that she had yet to remove.

'Pandora… I woke every morning this past week alone and surrounded by your scent. At first it made me angry, knowing you had left me. But as I calmed and your scent began to fade with every day…' He looked up, his eyes dark and earnest. 'I think it was while I burrowed my face into that damned pillow, trying to get one more breath of you… I think that was when I knew.'

'You knew that you wanted more?' she whispered, needing to clarify, needing to know exactly what he meant.

'So much more.' He lifted her hand to his lips, inhaling softly against her skin, breathing her in. 'I don't just want you in my bed for a week, *agape mou*. I was stupid to ever think that was all we could be. You are worth more to me than I could ever confine to one night, one week, or even one year.'

'Are you saying that you…?' She breathed in, feeling her heartbeat thrum so hard in her throat she felt a little dizzy. 'Xander… I need you to be clear before I…'

His eyes darkened. 'Before you what, Quinn?'

'Before I do something utterly ridiculous like jump your bones right here on this altar. It might not be a church but I'm pretty sure it would still be illegal.'

'Maybe I'll draw this speech out a little longer, then,' he mused.

Pandora fought the urge to playfully punch him like she wanted to, and took the final step, bringing them chest to chest so that she could look up into his eyes.

'I want to hear you say it again a few more times,' she said simply, fighting a smile so strong it made her cheeks ache with the sweetest pain. 'Then maybe I'll put you out of your misery.'

'If you want to divorce me right now, Pandora, I'll accept that, and I will throw every ounce of myself into wooing you for real. Because you are not just a name on a certificate to me, you're my everything. You're all that matters any more because I love you so much.'

She almost melted right then. Only she couldn't help teasing him a little more… 'You sure you don't want to keep that prenup?'

He winced, as if the memory of that day, of the words he'd thrown at her, caused him actual physical pain. 'I'd hoped to forget my behaviour.'

'Well, I don't.' She shook her head, noting the remorseful look in his eyes. 'You can't get to a happy ever after without a few moments of conflict along the way.'

He raised an eyebrow. 'Is that what we're calling the time I demanded that you marry me or I would have you carted off to jail?'

Pandora laughed and, after a moment of fighting it, her stern, serious husband laughed too. Then he scooped her up against his chest and kissed the last bubbles of mirth from her lips until she was boneless and sighing.

Emotion was hot and pulsing in her throat as she met his gaze, one hand reaching up to cup his jaw as she spoke those three beautiful words, cementing their vows all over again.

'I love you,' she whispered. 'I don't want a divorce. I don't care about any of the legal mumbo jumbo anyway. But I suppose we can't really tell our kids the story of our awful first wedding, can we?'

'Our kids?' He choked a little. 'You're think-ing about that already, are you?'

'Oh, not for a while yet. I have a five-year busi-ness plan to execute first, of course.' She smiled, a little laugh escaping her lips.

Xander laughed too, as if he too could hardly believe how things could feel this wonderful. It was fast, it was intense, and it was so completely, perfectly right.

'I have one last thing I'd like to do,' she whis-pered.

'Anything,' he breathed, holding her even tighter.

The first item on her list was to get her husband alone for a proper reunion, which turned out to be in the office of the grand house. Once the door had been locked, Xander proceeded to show her just how much he had missed her by spreading her out on top of the desk and promising to fulfil every fantasy about her sexy boss that she'd ever had. But in reality, neither of them had enough patience for that kind of lovemaking. Their union was simply frantic and raw, filled with whispers of love and the promise of a much slower explo-ration later.

Then, still naked and slightly sweaty from their efforts, she stepped away from him, tak-ing his hand and sliding the platinum band off his finger and clutching it in her fist. She did the same to her own and placed it in the centre of his palm. Meeting his eyes, she cleared her throat, praying she could get through this without dissolving into a sobbing pile of tears.

'Xander, I take you as my husband, I promise to love you and explore the world with you and remind you to relax when you're becoming a little too highly strung. For ever and always.' She placed the ring on his finger, surprised when she felt his hand shake a little.

He cleared his throat, taking a deep breath as he prepared to do the same. 'Pandora, I promise to love you and worship you and devotedly organise the itinerary for whatever far-flung corner of the world you decide to drag me to.'

Pandora tried to laugh, but the tears had already begun and all she managed was a little strangled sigh. He slid the ring onto her finger slowly, his eyes not leaving hers.

'Gia pánta kai pánta i agápi mou.' He repeated her words reverently in both of their languages. 'For ever and always.'

EPILOGUE

Four years later

PANDORA FELT SWEAT trickle down the centre of her back as she focused very hard on lowering herself into a nearby chair in the busy banquet area. The tiny baby she was holding wriggled quite a bit more than she'd anticipated and her upper arms had begun to ache.

'I'll only be gone for ten minutes at the most,' her sister-in-law Priya had said cheerfully as she brushed a lock of hair back on her daughter's jet-black curls. That had been twenty minutes ago and there was still no sign of her return from picking up her husband at the nearby dock.

Nor had there been a sign of her own husband during that time. She frowned, averting her gaze up for a moment to scan the open-air terrace of the large Greek villa. Other guests at the charity event milled around, sipping afternoon tea and networking. Xander had probably struck up a conversation with one of the countless European monarchs or global tycoons in attendance, she thought with a smile. He'd return triumphant, probably after negotiating a handful of deals.

But when she finally spotted him, he was quite alone, seated at a nearby table and unmistakeably focused on the very spot where she sat. Frowning, she did a small queen's wave, swaying her new niece gently in one arm. He nodded once and raised a glass of champagne in her direction, before rising and stalking purposefully towards her. His expression was strange, his eyes seeming to drink her in as he came closer before he stopped and reached out to touch his niece's chubby cheek.

The baby let out an instant gurgle of appreciation, grabbing onto her uncle's finger as if to stop him from leaving.

'If you tell me that this suits me, be prepared for me to roll my eyes,' Pandora said with a teasing smile.

'Okay, it doesn't suit you. You are the most unattractive sight I've ever seen, and I just sat at that table for the past five minutes staring at you...in sheer repulsion.' He leaned in to kiss her once, then twice for good measure before pulling back to stare once more.

He whispered something into the baby's ear conspiratorially, his eyes darting back up to meet hers dramatically. 'What's that, little one? You want to meet your baby cousin right now?'

She made an urgent shushing sound, looking around them. 'Xander, it's far too early to be talking about it in public.'

He ignored her, his eyes now apparently only for his little niece alone. 'I think it's a boy too. But it's okay. I'll keep going until we get you a girl cousin.'

'Oh, you will, will you?' Pandora couldn't help but grin as her husband's hand moved to splay across the still-flat expanse of her stomach. She had only just had a positive test days before.

'You're sure you don't want to tell anyone yet?' he asked, far too innocently. 'I know they say it's bad luck, but…'

'You are like a child, begging to unwrap his Christmas gift early. But no, I don't think I'm ready to share our news just yet.' She laughed, covering his hand with her own and feeling a brief intense burst of love for him and the tiny life growing steadily beneath their joint palms.

'I don't think I've ever even held a baby before today.' She frowned down at the little girl in her arms. Amara Theodorou blew a bubble and laughed, patting at the beads on Pandora's dress. 'I'm feeling a little out of my depth already.'

'I could tell by the stack of pregnancy books you packed in your overnight bag.'

Pandora looked away, feeling the ripples of uncertainty rise a little higher. She'd made no secret of her compulsion to study and prepare for every possibility of what lay ahead of her. But something about entering into this particular new phase of her life made her wish she were a more easy-going type. Perhaps if she could go with the flow, letting go of control of her body and life as she knew it wouldn't feel quite so terrifying.

'Hey, I wasn't making fun of your books.' Xander's palms touched her cheeks, applying gentle pressure and filling her with warmth. 'Once I saw them I actually downloaded some audio versions onto my phone. I've been learning all about the trimesters and stages on my morning runs.'

She paused, looking up into his face and taking a moment to gauge whether or not he was making fun of her. 'You've been studying too?'

'You're not the only one who likes to be prepared, *agape mou*. I have grand plans,' he murmured against her cheek.

'You can't win at fatherhood, Xander.' She smiled, feeling the tension ease within her ever so slightly. Trust her husband to turn parenthood into a competition with his brother.

She inhaled deeply, leaning forward to touch her forehead gently against his in silent communication of thanks. They had developed these small gestures over the years, tiny movements and touches that needed no words. She'd never dreamed of having such an easy connection with someone.

After a long moment, she looked up into his impossibly blue eyes and smiled, knowing he understood her worries and accepted them just as he accepted everything else about her. In their four years of marriage he'd kept his promise every single day, showing her that love didn't have to be something you earned or performed for. His love was unconditional and constant, and if there was one thing she could count on it was that Xander would throw himself into fatherhood with that same fierce strength and loyalty.

Warm lips touched hers and she smiled against his mouth, feeling a tentative spark of excitement bloom within her at the idea of them as parents. She'd never dreamed of this life for herself.

'We're in this together, remember?' Xander cupped her neck, kissing her once more. 'We can always ask my brother if we can take this little one again for practice.'

'Practice for what?' A familiar female voice spoke from behind Xander's shoulder. Priya appeared, her shrewd eyes homing in on their hushed conversation and lowering to where Xander's hand still rested. Pandora felt her facial muscles freeze a little as her brain struggled to formulate an excuse.

'Where is she?' Eros Theodorou appeared, his eyes scanning them all, and for a moment Pandora thought he was referring to her. But then his eyes lit up as they landed on his daughter and Amara was promptly scooped up into her father's arms.

Xander quickly worked his magic, distracting his brother and sister-in-law with some good-natured ribbing about their extended absence and obviously flushed cheeks but still Priya's eyes moved speculatively over her more than once.

As the conversation came to a momentary silence, Pandora felt the urge to share their news bubbling upwards until she couldn't hold it in any longer.

'I'm pregnant,' she blurted, much louder than she'd intended, instantly slamming a hand over her mouth. Priya's stunned smile was instantaneous, her hands clapping together with glee while Eros simply raised one brow in his brother's direction.

For a moment, the look of surprise on her husband's face made Pandora pause. She was poised to apologise for her own impulsive move but quickly felt the shudders of Xander's body crumpling into laughter beside her.

'And she was worried that I would let the news out.' His eyes creased as he was engulfed in a hug by Priya and then his younger brother, their embrace a thoroughly masculine movement of back-thumping and grunts but still a hug nonetheless.

Seeing Xander's relationship with his brother improve to this point had been something she'd never dreamed of, along with so many other wonderful developments that had happened in their family. Their unexpected joining of forces to take over the company had been an instant power pairing, with Eros's creativity and intuition coupling rather perfectly with Xander's intensity and ruthless precision in the boardroom. Together, they had cut out the rot left by their father and created something brand new that they could both be proud of.

Despite his refusal to enter into their deal, Nysio Bacchetti had eventually approached his two half-brothers with an offer that none of them could have predicted. But that was a story for another time.

'I think our secret won't be a secret for long.' She laughed as Xander continued to pull her away from the party towards where their helicopter lay in wait, whispering all the things he planned to do to help her relax.

'That does not sound very restful, husband dearest. In fact, it sounds quite the opposite.' She raised one brow as they paused under an archway of gloriously vibrant bougainvillea. 'I think we should plant some of these at the house… I wonder how long they take to grow…'

Xander barely flinched at her rapid change in topic. 'I'll order an acre of them.'

'And as for my credentials, I'll cite four years of studious observation and active research in ensuring the happiness of the woman I love.' He pulled her close so that their bodies met from chest to knee. 'I've come to the scientific conclusion that you are at your most relaxed when your mind and body are engaged and captivated…so I plan to spend the next eight months working very hard to achieve both.'

'You know me so well.' She smiled as he began kissing up her neck, holding her close in a tight embrace. This was all she needed, she realised with a throbbing lump in her throat. This man, this wonderful man and the life that lay nestled within her.

She no longer worried about where they would live if his work took them away, she simply focused on her own work and handed the reins to Xander, trusting him completely to take care of the details.

Xander's love had shored up all the holes in her own self-confidence, showing her how wonderful it could be to be accepted and loved, just as she was. That kind of unconditional love had run through her like a river until it wasn't just coming from him, it was from within too.

This newfound sense of strength seemed to interrupt every negative thought or moment of uncertainty she had, clearing her mind and helping her find better solutions. It was him. It was his love and unwavering belief that made her feel as if she could do anything. It was a heady feeling, being loved so much by such a force of a man.

As the helicopter lifted up into the air, she felt her husband's hand cover her own and their eyes met, an unspoken thrill of wonder and excitement passing between them. She smiled, realising they had always had this seamless connection, as though they were reading from the exact same page.

They might not have begun in the traditional fairy-tale fashion, but then again how many love stories ever did? This was her own perfectly imperfect storybook, and she had a feeling they had only just got started on building their happily-ever-after together.

* * * * *